PENGUIN CLASSICS
Maigret is Afraid

'Extraordinary masterpieces of the twentieth century'
John Banville

'A brilliant writer' — India Knight

'Intense atmosphere and resonant detail . . . make Simenon's
fiction remarkably like life' — Julian Barnes

'A truly wonderful writer . . . marvellously readable – lucid,
simple, absolutely in tune with the world he creates'
— Muriel Spark

'Few writers have ever conveyed with such a sure touch, the
bleakness of human life' — A. N. Wilson

'Compelling, remorseless, brilliant' — John Gray

'A writer of genius, one whose simplicity of language creates
indelible images that the florid stylists of our own day can
only dream of' — *Daily Mail*

'The mysteries of the human personality are revealed in all
their disconcerting complexity' — Anita Brookner

'One of the greatest writers of our time'
— *The Sunday Times*

'I love reading Simenon. He makes me think of Chekhov'
— William Faulkner

'One of the great psychological novelists of this century'
— *Independent*

'The greatest of all, the most genuine novelist we have had
in literature' — André Gide

'Simenon ought to be spoken of in the same breath as
Camus, Beckett and Kafka' — *Independent on Sunday*

Georges Simenon was born on 12 February 1903 in Liège, Belgium, and died in 1989 in Lausanne, Switzerland, where he had lived for the latter part of his life. Between 1931 and 1972 he published seventy-five novels and twenty-eight short stories featuring Inspector Maigret.

Simenon always resisted identifying himself with his famous literary character, but acknowledged that they shared an important characteristic:

> My motto, to the extent that I have one, has been noted often enough, and I've always conformed to it. It's the one I've given to old Maigret, who resembles me in certain points . . . 'understand and judge not'.

Penguin is publishing the entire series of Maigret novels.

GEORGES SIMENON

Maigret is Afraid

Translated by ROS SCHWARTZ

PENGUIN BOOKS

PENGUIN CLASSICS

UK | USA | Canada | Ireland | Australia
India | New Zealand | South Africa

Penguin Books is part of the Penguin Random House group of companies
whose addresses can be found at global.penguinrandomhouse.com

First published in French as *Maigret a peur* by Presses de la Cité 1953
This translation first published 2017

009

Set in Dante MT Std 12.5/15pt
Typeset in India by Thomson Digital Pvt Ltd, Noida, Delhi
Printed and bound in Great Britain by Clays Ltd, Elcograf S.p.A.

ISBN: 978-0-241-27748-5

www.greenpenguin.co.uk

Contents

1. A Train Journey in the Rain 1

2. The Rabbit-fur Seller 21

3. The School Teacher Who Never Slept 43

4. The Italian Woman with Bruises 64

5. The Game of Bridge 84

6. The Ten-thirty Mass 104

7. Louise's Treasure 125

8. The Invalid of Gros-Noyer 145

9. Vintage Napoleon Brandy 164

1. A Train Journey in the Rain

All of a sudden, between two small stations whose names he didn't know and of which he could see almost nothing in the dark, apart from the slashing rain in the beam of a large lamp and human shapes pushing carts, Maigret wondered what he was doing there.

Perhaps he'd dozed off for a moment in the overheated compartment? He couldn't have lost consciousness entirely because he knew he was on a train – he could hear its steady chugging. He would have sworn that he'd occasionally seen the lit windows of an isolated farmhouse dotted among the dark expanses of countryside. All these things were real, as were the smell of soot mingled with that of his damp clothes and the regular murmur of voices from an adjacent compartment, but everything had somehow lost its immediacy, it could no longer be located in space or, more specifically, in time.

He could have been elsewhere, in any dinky train travelling across the countryside, and he could have been a fifteen-year-old Maigret coming home from school on a Saturday, on a local train exactly like this one, with old-fashioned carriages whose partitions creaked as the engine strained. There would be the same voices in the dark at each stop, the same men busying themselves around the mail compartment, the same stationmaster's whistle.

He half-opened his eyes, puffed on his pipe, which had gone out, and his gaze lighted on the man sitting in the opposite corner of the compartment. He could have been a passenger on the train that once used to take Maigret to his father's. He could have been the count or the owner of the château, the dignitary of a village or of any small town.

He wore a light tweed golfing suit and the sort of raincoat that is sold only in very expensive shops. He had a green hunting hat, with a tiny pheasant plume tucked under the ribbon. Despite the heat, he hadn't taken off his fawn gloves, for those people never remove their gloves on a train or in a car. And, despite the rain, there wasn't a spot of mud on his immaculately shiny shoes.

He looked about sixty-five. An elderly gentleman. Isn't it curious how men of that age pay so much attention to every detail of their appearance? And how they still like to pretend they are different from common mortals?

His complexion was the pink that is peculiar to his kind, and he had a thin silver-white moustache stained yellow from smoking cigars.

His gaze, however, did not contain all the assurance one might have expected. From his corner, the man was watching Maigret who, meanwhile, darted little glances in his direction and twice or three times looked on the verge of saying something. The train set off again, grimy and wet, into a dark world punctuated by scattered lights. Sometimes, at a level-crossing, you could just make out a person on a bicycle waiting for the convoy to pass.

Was Maigret sad? It was a more nebulous mood. He wasn't feeling completely at ease with himself. And for a start, he had drunk too much these past three days, but it had been an obligation, not a pleasure.

He was on his way back from the international police congress in Bordeaux. It was April. When he had left Paris, where the winter had been long and dreary, it had felt as if spring was around the corner. But, in Bordeaux, it had rained non-stop for three days, with a cold wind that plastered your clothes to your body.

It so happened that the few friends he usually met at these congresses, like Mr Pyke, were not there. Each country seemed to have contrived to send only youngsters, men of thirty to forty who were new faces. They had all been very kind to him, very deferential, as people are towards an elder they respect but consider a bit out of touch.

Was it all a figment of his imagination, or had the never-ending rain made him grumpy? Or was it all the wine they'd had to drink at the wineries they had visited at the invitation of the Chamber of Commerce?

'Are you having a good time?' his wife had asked him on the telephone.

He had replied with a groan.

'Try and have a bit of a rest. You looked tired when you left. Anyway, it will be a change of scene. Don't catch cold.'

Perhaps he was suddenly feeling old? Not even the discussions, which had nearly all been about new scientific techniques, had interested him.

The dinner had been held the previous evening. That morning there had been a closing reception, at the town hall this time, and a lunch washed down with copious amounts of wine. He had promised Chabot that he would take advantage of the fact that he didn't have to be in Paris until the Monday morning to drop in and see him in Fontenay-le-Comte.

Chabot wasn't getting any younger either. They had been friends long ago, when Maigret had been a medical student for two years at Nantes University. Chabot had been studying law. They had shared lodgings. On two or three occasions, on a Sunday, he had gone with his friend to visit his mother in Fontenay.

And since then, over the years, they had seen each other maybe ten times in all.

'When are you going to come and look me up in Vendée?'

Madame Maigret had encouraged him.

'Why don't you go and see your friend Chabot on the way back from Bordeaux?'

He should have arrived in Fontenay two hours ago, but he had taken the wrong train. In Niort, where he had waited for ages, drinking small glasses of wine in the waiting room, he had been tempted to telephone Chabot to ask him to drive over and pick him up.

But he hadn't done so in the end because, if Julien came to fetch him, he would insist on his staying the night, and Maigret hated sleeping in other people's houses.

He would go to a hotel and telephone only once he was settled in. He had been wrong to make this detour instead of spending these two days' holiday at home, on Boulevard Richard-Lenoir. Who knows? Maybe it wasn't raining in Paris and spring had finally arrived.

'So they've brought you down here . . .'

He gave a start. Without realizing it, he must have continued vaguely staring at his travelling companion, who had just made up his mind to speak to him. This seemed to be causing him some embarrassment and he felt obliged to add a note of irony to his words.

'I beg your pardon?'

'I said I was certain they'd turn to someone like you.'

Then, since Maigret still looked bemused:

'You are Detective Chief Inspector Maigret, aren't you?'

The passenger became a man of the world again and rose from the banquette to introduce himself:

'Vernoux de Courçon.'

'Pleased to meet you.'

'I recognized you immediately from having seen your photograph in the newspapers.'

From the way he said it, he sounded as if he were apologizing for being someone who read the papers.

'It must happen often.'

'What?'

'That people recognize you.'

Maigret didn't know what to reply. He hadn't come fully back down to earth yet. There were beads of sweat on the man's forehead, as if he had put himself in a situation from which he didn't know how to extricate himself.

'Was it my friend Julien who telephoned you?'

'Do you mean Julien Chabot?'

'The investigating magistrate. What surprises me is that he said nothing to me about it when I saw him this morning.'

'I still don't understand.'

Vernoux de Courçon studied him more closely, frowning.

'Are you saying it's coincidence that brings you to Fontenay-le-Comte?'

'Yes.'

'You're not on your way to Julien Chabot's?'

'I am, but . . .'

Maigret suddenly blushed, furious with himself, because he had just answered meekly, as he had done in the past with people like the man facing him, 'the upper crust'.

'Odd, isn't it?' said Vernoux de Courçon, wryly.

'What is odd?'

'That Detective Chief Inspector Maigret, who has probably never set foot in Fontenay—'

'Is that what you've been told?'

'I presume so. In any case, we haven't seen you there often and I've never heard mention of any visits. I was saying it's odd that you turn up just when the authorities are having to deal with the most perplexing mystery that . . .'

Maigret struck a match and gave little puffs on his pipe.

'Julien Chabot and I were students together for a while,' he said calmly. 'In the past, I was an occasional guest at his home in Rue Clemenceau.'

'Really?'

Taciturnly, he echoed:

'Really.'

'In that case, we'll probably see one another tomorrow evening at my house, Rue Rabelais. Chabot comes every Saturday to play bridge.'

The train stopped one last time before Fontenay. Vernoux de Courçon had no luggage, only a brown leather briefcase lying next to him on the seat.

'I'm intrigued to know whether you will solve the mystery. Coincidence or not, it's lucky for Chabot that you are here.'

'Is his mother still alive?'

'As hale and hearty as ever.'

The man rose to button up his raincoat, stretch his gloves and adjust his hat. The train was slowing down, lights flashed past more frequently and people on the platform started running.

'Delighted to have met you. Tell Chabot I hope you'll join him tomorrow evening.'

Maigret merely nodded in reply, opened the compartment door, grabbed his suitcase, which was heavy, and made for the train door without looking at the people he passed.

Chabot couldn't be expecting him on that train, which he had only taken by chance. From the station entrance, Maigret could see all the way down Rue de la République, where it was raining even harder.

'Taxi, sir?'

He nodded.

'Hôtel de France?'

He replied yes again and slumped in the back of the cab, feeling irritable. It was only nine o'clock in the evening, but the town was dead, and only two or three cafés still had their lights on. The door of the Hôtel de France was flanked by two palm trees in green barrels.

'Do you have a room?'

'For one?'

'Yes. And if possible I'd like something to eat.'

The hotel had already closed for the night, like a church after vespers. The receptionist had to go and check with the kitchen. He turned on two or three lamps in the dining room.

Maigret washed his hands at a porcelain basin to avoid having to go up to his room.

'White wine?'

He was nauseated by all the white wine he had been obliged to drink in Bordeaux.

'Do you have any beer?'

'Only bottled.'

'Then give me a decent red.'

They heated up some soup for him and sliced some ham. From where he was sitting, he saw someone enter the lobby, dripping wet. Finding no one at the desk, the newcomer glanced around the dining room and looked relieved on spotting Maigret. Aged around forty, he had ginger hair and plump red cheeks, and cameras were slung over the shoulders of his beige raincoat.

He shook the rain from his hat and came into the room.

'First of all, may I take a photo? I'm the regional correspondent from the *Ouest-Éclair*. I saw you at the station, but I wasn't able to catch you. So they've asked you to come and shed light on the Courçon case.'

A flash. A click.

'Inspector Féron didn't tell us about you. Nor did the investigating magistrate.'

'I am not here for the Courçon case.'

The ginger-haired journalist smiled the smile of a hack who is not fooled.

'Of course not!'

'What do you mean, "of course not"?'

'You're not here *officially*. I get it. All the same—'

'All the same, nothing!'

'The proof is that Féron told me he's on his way.'

'Who is Féron?'

'Fontenay's police chief. When I spotted you at the station, I ran over to the telephone booth and called him. He said he'd meet me here.'

'*Here?*'

'Of course. Where else would you be staying?'

Maigret drained his glass, wiped his mouth and muttered:

'Who is this Vernoux de Courçon with whom I travelled from Niort?'

'He was indeed on that train. He's the brother-in-law.'

'Whose brother-in-law?'

'Of the De Courçon who's been murdered.'

A short figure with brown hair now came into the hotel and made a beeline for the two men in the dining room.

'Hello, Féron!' said the journalist.

'Hello, you. My apologies, detective chief inspector. No one told me you were coming, which is why I wasn't at the station. I was having a bite to eat, after an exhausting day, when—'

He jerked his head in the journalist's direction.

'I raced over and—'

'I was saying to this young man,' replied Maigret, pushing away his plate and picking up his pipe, 'that I have nothing to do with your Courçon case. I'm in Fontenay-le-Comte through the greatest of coincidences, to say hello to my good old friend Chabot and—'

'Does he know you're here?'

'He must have been expecting me on the four o'clock train. When he saw I wasn't on it, he probably assumed I'd only be coming tomorrow or that I wouldn't be coming at all.'

Maigret stood up.

'And now, if you'll excuse me, I'm going to drop in and say hello before I go to bed.'

The police chief and the reporter both looked equally disconcerted.

'Do you really know nothing?'

'Absolutely nothing.'

'You haven't read the papers?'

'For the past three days, the congress organizers and the Bordeaux Chamber of Commerce ensured that we didn't have the leisure.'

They exchanged sceptical glances.

'Do you know where Chabot lives?'

'Of course I do. Unless the town has changed since I was last here.'

They couldn't bring themselves to let him go. Outside on the pavement, they lingered beside him.

'Gentlemen, I wish you goodnight.'

The reporter pressed him:

'Do you have anything to say to the *Ouest-Éclair*?'

'Nothing. Goodnight, gentlemen.'

He reached Rue de la République, crossed the bridge and passed only two people on his way to Chabot's. His friend lived in an old house which had once been the envy of the young Maigret. It was still the same, built of grey stone with four steps up to the front door, and tall windows. A little light filtered through the gap in the curtains. He rang the bell and heard footsteps on the blue tiles in the hall. A spy hole in the door opened.

'Is Monsieur Chabot at home?' he asked.

'Who is it?'

'Inspector Maigret.'

'Is that you, Monsieur Maigret?'

He recognized the voice of Rose, the Chabots' servant, who was already with them thirty years earlier.

'I'll let you in right away. Just wait while I undo the chain.'

As she did so, she shouted into the house:

'Monsieur Julien! It's your friend Monsieur Maigret . . . Come in, Monsieur Maigret . . . Monsieur Julien went to the station this afternoon . . . He was disappointed when you didn't show up. How did you get here?'

'By train.'

'You mean the local evening train?'

A door had opened. Standing in the shaft of orange light was a tall, thin, slightly stooped figure in a brown-velvet smoking jacket.

'Is that you?' he said.

'Of course it is. I missed the fast train, so I took the slow one.'

'Your luggage?'

'It's at the hotel.'

'Are you mad? I'll have to send for it. We agreed that you would stay here.'

'Now look, Julien . . .'

It was funny. He had to force himself to call his old friend by his first name and it sounded odd. It didn't come naturally to be familiar with him.

'Come in! I hope you haven't had dinner?'

'I have. At the Hôtel de France.'

'Shall I inform Madame?' asked Rose.

Maigret interrupted.

'I imagine she's in bed?'

'She's just gone upstairs. But she doesn't go to bed before eleven o'clock or midnight. I—'

'No. I forbid you to disturb her. I'll see your mother tomorrow morning.'

'She won't be happy.'

Maigret calculated that Madame Chabot must be at least seventy-eight. He was secretly wishing he hadn't come. But all the same he hung his rain-sodden overcoat on the antique coat rack and followed Julien into his study, while Rose, who was over sixty herself, waited for orders.

'What will you have? A vintage brandy?'

'If you like.'

Rose understood the magistrate's unspoken instructions and left the room. The smell of the house hadn't changed and that was something else that Maigret had once envied, the smell of a well-kept home, where the wooden floors are polished and the food is good.

He would have sworn that every single piece of furniture was in the same place.

'Do sit down. It's good to see you . . .'

He would have been tempted to say that Chabot hadn't changed either. He recognized his features, his expression. Since they had both aged, Maigret barely realized that the years had taken their toll. All the same, he was struck by something gloomy, hesitant, slightly feeble, that he had never noticed in his friend before.

Had he been like that in the past? Was it that Maigret hadn't noticed?

'Cigar?'

There was a stack of boxes on the mantelpiece.

'I always smoke a pipe.'

'It's true. I'd forgotten. I myself haven't smoked for twelve years.'

'Doctor's orders?'

'No. One fine day, I said to myself that it was stupid to make smoke and . . .'

Rose came in with a tray on which there was a bottle covered with a fine film of dust from the cellar and a single crystal glass.

'You don't drink any more either?'

'I gave up at the same time. Just a little watered-down wine at mealtimes. As for you, you haven't changed.'

'You think?'

'You appear to be enjoying excellent health. It really is a pleasure to see you.'

Why did he not sound entirely sincere?

'You've promised to visit these parts and then cried off at the last minute so often that I confess I wasn't really expecting you.'

'But here I am, aren't I? You see!'

'Your wife?'

'She's well.'

'She didn't come with you?'

'She doesn't like congresses.'

'Did it go well?'

'We drank a lot, talked a lot, ate a lot.'

'Myself, I travel less and less.'

He lowered his voice because footsteps could be heard upstairs.

'It's difficult with my mother. Besides, I can't leave her on her own any more.'

'Is she still as robust?'

'She hasn't changed. Only her eyesight is deteriorating a little. It upsets her not to be able to thread her needles, but she refuses to wear glasses.'

It was obvious that his mind was elsewhere as he looked at Maigret rather in the same way as Vernoux de Courçon had stared at him in the train.

'Have you heard?'

'About what?'

'About what's going on here.'

'I haven't read the papers for almost a week. But I travelled earlier with a certain Vernoux de Courçon who claims to be your friend.'

'Hubert?'

'I don't know. A man of around sixty-five.'

'That's Hubert.'

There was no sound coming from the town. You could only hear the patter of rain beating against the windowpanes and, from time to time, the crackling of the logs in the hearth. In his day, Julien Chabot's father had been an investigating magistrate in Fontenay-le-Comte and the study hadn't changed since his son had taken it over.

'In that case, people must have told you—'

'Almost nothing. A journalist with a camera cornered me in the hotel dining room.'

'A redhead?'

'Yes.'

'That's Lomel. What did he say to you?'

'He was convinced I was here to handle some case. I didn't have the time to disabuse him before the police chief turned up too.'

'In short, right now, the entire town knows you're here?'

'Does that bother you?'

Chabot just managed to conceal his hesitation.

'No . . . except that . . .'

'Except that what?'

'Nothing. It's very complicated. You've never lived in a small town like Fontenay.'

'I lived in Luçon for more than a year, you know!'

'There was never a case like the one I've got on my hands.'

'I remember a certain murder, in L'Aiguillon . . .'

'That's true. I was forgetting.'

Maigret was referring to a case where he had been obliged to arrest a former magistrate, universally considered to be utterly respectable, for murder.

'At least it's not as bad as that. You'll find out tomorrow morning. I'd be surprised if the journalists from Paris didn't arrive on the first train.'

'A murder?'

'Two.'

'Vernoux de Courçon's brother-in-law?'

'You see, you do know about it!'

'That's all I've heard.'

'His brother-in-law, yes, Robert de Courçon, who was killed four days ago. That alone would have been enough to cause a scandal. The day before yesterday, it was the widow Gibon's turn.'

'Who is she?'

'No one of importance. Quite the opposite. An old woman who lived alone at the far end of Rue des Loges.'

'What's the connection between the two murders?'

'They were both committed in the same way, probably with the same weapon.'

'A revolver?'

'No. A blunt object, as we say in police reports. A section of lead piping, or a tool like a monkey wrench.'

'Is that all?'

'Isn't it enough? . . . Sssh!'

The door opened noiselessly and a tiny, thin woman dressed in black walked in, her hand extended.

'It's you, Jules!'

How many years had it been since anyone had called him by his first name?

'My son went to the station. When he came back he told me you wouldn't be coming now and I went upstairs. Haven't you been given anything to eat?'

'He had dinner at the hotel, Mother.'

'What do you mean, at the hotel?'

'He's staying at the Hôtel de France. He refuses to—'

'I won't hear of it! I will not allow you to . . .'

'Believe me, madame, it is much better that I stay at the hotel because the news hounds are already after me. If I were to accept your invitation, tomorrow morning, if not tonight, they'd be ringing your bell non-stop. In fact, it would be better not to say that I'm here at the invitation of your son . . .'

So that was what was bothering the magistrate, and Maigret saw the confirmation written on his face.

'People will still say that you are!'

'I'll deny it. This case, or rather these cases, are none of my concern. I have no intention of getting involved.'

Was Chabot afraid that he would get mixed up in something that was none of his business? Or was he worried that Maigret, with his sometimes rather idiosyncratic methods, could put him in a delicate situation?

Maigret had turned up at a bad time.

'I wonder, Mother, whether Maigret mightn't be right.'

And, turning towards his old friend:

'This is no ordinary investigation, you see. Robert de Courçon, the man who was murdered, was well known, and related in one way or another to all the prominent families in the region. His brother-in-law Vernoux is also a leading figure. After the first murder, rumours began to circulate. Then the widow Gibon was killed, and that changed the nature of the speculation somewhat. But . . .'

'But . . .?'

'It's hard to explain. The police chief is in charge of the investigation. He's a good man, who knows the town, even though he's from the south, from Arles, I think. The Poitiers Flying Squad's on the scene too. As far as I'm concerned . . .'

The old lady had sat down on the edge of a chair as if she were a visitor, and was listening to her son talk as if listening to the sermon at high mass.

'Two murders in three days, that's a lot for a town with a population of eight thousand. People are getting scared. It's not just because of the rain that there's no one out and about tonight.'

'What do people think?'

'Some reckon it's a madman.'

'Nothing was stolen?'

'Not in either case. And in both instances the murderer gained entry to the house without arousing the victim's suspicion. That's a clue. It's more or less the only one we have.'

'No fingerprints?'

'None. If it is a madman, he'll probably strike again.'

'I see. What about you, what do you think?'

'Nothing. I'm trying to find out. There's something bothering me.'

'What?'

'It's still too vague for me to be able to explain. I have a huge responsibility on my shoulders.'

He said that like an overburdened official. And it was very much an official that Maigret now had in front of him, an official from a small town, living in dread of making a mistake.

Had Maigret become like that with age too? Because of his friend, he felt himself growing old.

'I wonder whether it might be best for me to take the first train to Paris. I only came to Fontenay to say hello to you. I've done that. My presence here is likely to make things difficult for you.'

'What do you mean?'

Chabot's instinctive reaction had not been to protest.

'Already the redhead and the police chief are convinced that you asked me to come to the rescue. People will say that you're afraid, that you don't know how to deal with it, that—'

'Not at all.'

The magistrate half-heartedly dismissed that idea.

'I won't allow you to leave. I'm entitled to receive visits from my friends when I so wish.'

'My son is right, Jules. And I think you should come and stay with us.'

'Maigret prefers to be free to come and go as he pleases, don't you, Maigret?'

'I have my little ways.'

'I shan't press you.'

'I still think it would be for the best if I left tomorrow morning.'

Was Chabot about to concur? The telephone rang and the sound wasn't the same as normal telephones; this one had an old-fashioned ring.

'Would you excuse me?'

Chabot picked up the receiver.

'Investigating Magistrate Chabot speaking.'

The way he said that was another signal, and Maigret tried hard to suppress a smile.

'Who? . . . Oh! Yes . . . Go ahead, Féron . . . What? . . . Gobillard? . . . Where? . . . On the corner of Champ-de-Mars and Rue . . . I'm on my way . . . Yes . . . He's here . . . I don't know . . . Don't let anyone touch anything until I get there . . .'

His mother watched him, one hand on her chest.

'Another one?' she gasped.

He nodded.

'Gobillard.'

He explained to Maigret:

'An old drunkard who everyone in Fontenay knows because he spends most of his time fishing near the bridge. He's just been found dead in the street.'

'Murdered?'

'His skull smashed, like the other two, probably with the same instrument.'

He sprang to his feet, opened the door and took an old trenchcoat from the rack and a battered hat, which he probably only wore when it was raining.

'Are you coming?'

'Are you sure that I should go with you?'

'Now everyone knows you're here, people will wonder why I haven't brought you. Two murders was already a lot. With a third, people will be terrified.'

Just as they were leaving, a nervous little hand tugged Maigret's sleeve and the elderly mother whispered to him:

'Keep an eye on him, Jules! He's so conscientious that he doesn't realize the danger he's in.'

2. The Rabbit-fur Seller

The weather was so contrary and fierce that the rain wasn't mere rain or the wind freezing wind – this was a conspiracy of the elements. Earlier, standing on Niort station's exposed platform, fatigued by this relentless winter that was dragging on and on, Maigret had been reminded of a wounded animal that won't die and is determined to keep biting to the very end.

There was no point trying to protect himself. Water wasn't just pelting down from the sky but was also dripping from the guttering, in fat, cold drops, streaming down the doors of the houses and racing along the gutters with the gurgling of a torrent; you had water all over your face and neck, in your shoes and even in the pockets of your clothes, which were impossible to dry between two sallies outdoors.

They walked in the teeth of the wind, without speaking, straining forwards, the magistrate in his old raincoat that was flapping like a flag, Maigret in his overcoat, which weighed a ton. After a few steps, the tobacco in his pipe went out with a sizzling sound.

They saw the occasional lighted window, but not many. After the bridge, they passed the windows of the Café de la Poste and were aware that people were watching from behind the curtains; the door opened after they had gone by and they heard footsteps and voices.

The murder had taken place very near to that spot. In Fontenay, nothing is ever very far away and there is generally no need to use a car. A little street turned off to the right, connecting Rue de la République and the Champ-de-Mars. People were clustered outside the third or fourth house, close to the lights of an ambulance, some of them holding torches.

A short man broke away from the group, Inspector Féron, who almost committed the gaffe of addressing Maigret instead of Chabot.

'I telephoned you right away, from the Café de la Poste. I also called the prosecutor.'

A human form lay on the pavement, one hand in the gutter, pale skin visible between his black shoes and the bottoms of his trousers: Gobillard, the dead man, was wearing no socks. His hat lay a metre away. The inspector shone his torch in his face and, as Maigret and Chabot both leaned over, there was a flash, a click, then the voice of the ginger-haired journalist asking:

'One more please. Go closer, Monsieur Maigret.'

Maigret stepped back, muttering. Two or three onlookers stood close to the body, gawping at it, then at a good distance, five or six metres away, was a second, larger group, with people talking in hushed voices.

Chabot asked questions in a tone that was both official and exasperated:

'Who found him?'

And Féron replied, pointing to one of the closest figures: 'Doctor Vernoux.'

Was he from the same family as the man on the train? As far as it was possible to tell in the dark, he looked a lot younger.

Thirty-five perhaps? He was tall, with a long, animated face, and wore glasses, which had rain running down them.

He and Chabot shook hands automatically, like men who see one another every day or even several times a day.

The doctor explained softly:

'I was on my way to a friend's house on the other side of the square. I saw something on the pavement. I bent down. He was already dead. To save time, I ran into the Café de la Poste and telephoned the chief inspector.'

One by one, other faces appeared in the torch beams, all behind a veil of slanting rain.

'Are you here, Jussieux?'

Handshake. These people knew each other as well as classmates.

'I happened to be in the café. We were playing bridge and we all came . . .'

The magistrate remembered Maigret, who was standing to one side, and introduced him:

'Doctor Jussieux, a friend. Detective Chief Inspector Maigret . . .'

Jussieux explained:

'Same method as for the other two. A violent blow to the crown of the head. The weapon slipped slightly to the left this time. Gobillard too was attacked from the front, and he didn't attempt to protect himself in any way.'

'Drunk?'

'You only need to bend over and sniff. You know what he's usually like at this hour . . .'

Maigret was only half-listening. Lomel, the ginger-haired reporter, who had just taken a second photo, was trying to draw him aside. The thing that struck Maigret was quite hard to define.

The smaller of the two groups, the one closest to the body, seemed to be made up only of people who knew one another and belonged to a particular milieu: the magistrate, the two doctors, probably the men who had been playing bridge earlier with Doctor Jussieux and were doubtless all local bigwigs.

The other, less illustrious group did not maintain the same silence. Without overtly showing it, they exuded a certain hostility. There were even a few sniggers.

A dark car drew up behind the ambulance and a man alighted, stopping short on recognizing Maigret.

'You're here, chief!'

He did not seem overjoyed to see Maigret. This was Chabiron, a Flying Squad inspector on secondment to the Poitiers force for the past few years.

'So they've brought you in?'

'I'm here by chance.'

'That's what's known as a happy coincidence, isn't it?'

He also sniggered.

'I was driving around, patrolling the town, which is why it took a while to get hold of me. Who is it?'

Féron, the police chief, told him:

'A certain Gobillard, a fellow who does the rounds of Fontenay once or twice a week collecting rabbit skins. He also buys cow hides and sheep skins from the municipal abattoir. He has a cart and an old horse and lives in a shack outside town. He spends most of his time fishing by the bridge, using the most disgusting bait – bone marrow, chicken guts, congealed blood . . .'

Chabiron must have been an angler.

'Does he ever catch any fish?'

'He's about the only one who ever does. In the evening, he goes from bar to bar, knocking back a glass of red in each one until he's had enough.'

'Never any trouble?'

'Never.'

'Married?'

'He lives alone with his horse and a huge number of cats.'

Chabiron turned to Maigret:

'What do you think, chief?'

'I don't think anything.'

'Three in one week isn't bad for a godforsaken place like this.'

'What do we do with him?' Féron asked the magistrate.

'I don't think we need to wait for the prosecutor. Wasn't he at home?'

'No. His wife is trying to get hold of him on the telephone.'

'I think the body can be taken to the morgue.'

He turned to Doctor Vernoux.

'You didn't see or hear anything else, I assume?'

'Nothing. I was walking quickly, with my hands in my pockets. I almost tripped over him.'

'Is your father at home?'

'He came back from Niort this evening; he was having dinner when I left.'

As far as Maigret could gather, he was the son of Vernoux de Courçon, his travelling companion earlier on the slow train.

'You can take him away, boys.'

The reporter wouldn't leave Maigret in peace.

'Are you going to handle things now?'

'Certainly not.'

'Not even privately?'

'No.'

'Aren't you intrigued?'

'No.'

'Do you also think it's the work of a madman?'

Chabot and Doctor Vernoux, who had overheard, exchanged glances, still with that air of belonging to the same set, of knowing one another so well that there was no need for words.

This was natural. It is the same everywhere. But Maigret had rarely experienced such cliqueyness. In a small town such as this, of course, the dignitaries are few and inevitably meet each other several times a day, even if it is only in the street.

Then there are the others, like those who stood huddled on the sidelines looking disgruntled.

Without Maigret asking him anything, Inspector Chabiron volunteered:

'Two of us have come. Levras, who was with me, had to leave this morning because his wife is about to give birth any minute now. I'm doing my best. I'm trying every angle of the case at once. But as for getting these people to talk . . .'

It was the first group, the bigwigs, that he indicated with a jerk of his chin. His sympathies were clearly with the others.

'The police chief is also doing his utmost. He only has four officers. They've been working all day. How many have you got on patrol right now, Féron?'

'Three.'

As if to confirm his words, a uniformed cyclist stopped by the kerb and shook the rain from his shoulders.

'Nothing?'

'I checked the identities of the half-dozen or so people I met. I'll give you the list. They all had a good reason to be out and about.'

'Will you come back to my place for a moment?' Chabot asked Maigret.

He hesitated. If he went, it was because he needed a drink to warm himself up and he didn't expect to be able to find one at the hotel.

'I'll walk with you,' announced Doctor Vernoux. 'Unless I'm intruding?'

'Not at all.'

This time the wind was behind them and they were able to talk. The ambulance had driven off with Gobillard's body and its red tail light could be seen near Place Viète.

'I haven't introduced you properly. Vernoux is the son of Hubert Vernoux, whom you met on the train. He studied medicine but is not a practitioner, he is chiefly interested in research.'

'Research!' protested the doctor vaguely.

'He was a junior doctor at Sainte-Anne for two years. He developed a keen interest in psychiatry and visits the Niort insane asylum two or three times a week.'

'Do you think these three murders are the work of a madman?' asked Maigret, more out of politeness than anything else.

What he had just been told did not make him warm to Vernoux because he had little time for amateurs.

'It is more than likely, if not certain.'

'Do you know any madmen in Fontenay?'

'There are mad people everywhere, but generally they are discovered only when they go berserk.'

'I don't suppose it could be a woman?'

'Why not?'

'Because of the force with which all three victims were hit. It can't be easy to kill three times in that manner, without ever having to strike twice.'

'First of all, a lot of women are as strong as men. Secondly, when it comes to the insane . . .'

They had already reached the house.

'Anything to add, Vernoux?'

'Not for the time being.'

'Will I see you tomorrow?'

'Almost certainly.'

Chabot rummaged in his pocket for the key. In the hall, he and Maigret stamped their feet to shake the rain from their clothes, making puddles on the tiled floor. The two women, the mother and the servant, were waiting in a small, gloomy sitting room looking on to the street.

'You can go to bed, Mother. There's nothing else we can do tonight other than ask the gendarmerie to send all their available men out on patrol.'

She eventually decided to go upstairs.

'I'm really embarrassed that you're not staying with us, Jules!'

'I promise you that if I stay longer than twenty-four hours here, which I doubt, I'll avail myself of your hospitality.'

They were back in the timeless study, where the bottle of brandy was still in its place. Maigret poured himself a drink and went and stood with his back to the fire, glass in hand.

He could tell that Chabot was ill at ease, and that it was the reason he had invited him back. But first of all, the magistrate telephoned the gendarmerie.

'Is that you, lieutenant? Were you asleep? I'm sorry to disturb you at this hour . . .'

A clock with a bronze face on which the hands were barely visible showed half past eleven.

'Another one, yes . . . Gobillard . . . In the street, this time . . . And from the front, yes . . . He's already been taken to the morgue . . . Jussieux must be in the middle of doing the autopsy, but I doubt it'll tell us anything new . . . Do you have any men to hand? . . . I think it would be a good idea for them to patrol the town, not so much tonight as from first thing tomorrow, so as to reassure people . . . You understand? . . . Yes . . . I felt it earlier too . . . Thank you, lieutenant.'

Hanging up, he muttered:

'A charming fellow, who spent some time in Saumur . . .'

He must have realized what that meant – another reference to a clique! – and he reddened a little.

'You see! I'm doing my best. This must seem childlike to you. You probably think we're fighting with toy guns. But we don't have an organization like the one you're used to in Paris. Take fingerprints, for instance – each time I have to call in an expert from Poitiers. The same with everything else. The local police are more accustomed to petty offences than murder. As for the squad from Poitiers, they don't know the people of Fontenay . . .'

After a silence, he went on:

'I so wish I didn't have a case like this to deal with three years before I retire. Actually, we're around the same age. You too, in three years' time . . .'

'Me too.'

'Do you have any plans?'

'I've even bought a little house in the country, on the banks of the Loire.'

'You'll be bored.'

'Are you bored here?'

'It's not the same thing. I was born here. My father was born here. I know everyone.'

'The townsfolk don't seem happy.'

'You've only just arrived and you've already sensed that? You're right. I think it's inevitable. One murder, fair enough. Especially the first one.'

'Why?'

'Because it was Robert de Courçon.'

'Was he disliked?'

Chabot did not answer straight away. He seemed to be choosing his words first.

'To be honest, the people in the street didn't really know him other than in passing.'

'Married? Children?'

'An old bachelor. An eccentric, but a good man. If he'd been the only one, people would have been fairly indifferent. Just the little excitement that a murder always arouses. But on top of that one, there was the old Gibon woman and now Gobillard. Tomorrow, I'm expecting—'

'It's begun.'

'What?'

'The group that was standing to one side, the people from the street, I suppose, and those who came out of the Café de la Poste, looked the most hostile to me.'

'It's not as bad as all that. But—'

'Is the town very left-wing?'

'Yes and no. That's not exactly it either.'

'The Vernoux aren't popular?'

'Is that what you were told?'

Playing for time, Chabot asked:

'Won't you sit down? Another drink? I'm going to try and explain. It's not easy. You know Vendée, even if only by repute. For a long time, the people who were gossiped about were the château owners, counts, viscounts, minor aristocrats who kept to themselves and formed a closed society. There are still a few left, nearly all of them ruined, and they are no longer of any importance. But some of them continue to put on airs and graces. Do you understand?'

'It's the same everywhere in the countryside.'

'Now, others have taken their place.'

'Vernoux?'

'You've met him. Guess what his father used to do.'

'I haven't the faintest idea! How do you expect . . .?'

'Livestock dealer. The grandfather was a farmhand. Old Vernoux used to buy the animals locally and take them to Paris, entire herds, on the roads. He made a lot of money. He was a brute, always half-drunk, and died of *delirium tremens*, incidentally. His son—'

'Hubert? The man on the train?'

'Yes. They sent him to college. I think he went to university for a year. In his old age, the father started buying farms and land as well as livestock, and that's the profession Hubert took up.'

'So he's an estate agent.'

'Yes. His offices are near the station. The big stone house, that's where he lived before he got married.'

'Did he marry into money?'

'In a way, yes. But not entirely. She was a Courçon. Are you interested?'

'Of course!'

'It will give you a better picture of the town. The Courçons were actually called Courçon-Lagrange. Originally, they were simply Lagrange. They added Courçon to their name when they bought the Château de Courçon. That was three or four generations back. I can't remember what the founder of the dynasty used to sell. Livestock as well, probably, or scrap iron. But that was forgotten by the time Hubert Vernoux appeared. The children and grandchildren no longer work. Robert de Courçon, the man who was murdered, was accepted into the aristocracy and he was the local expert on heraldry. He wrote several books on the subject. He had two sisters, Isabelle and Lucile. Isabelle married Vernoux, who immediately started signing his name as Vernoux de Courçon. Are you with me?'

'It's not too difficult! I imagine that at the time of that marriage, the Courçons had fallen on hard times and were penniless?'

'More or less. They still had a mortgaged château in the forest of Mervent and the mansion in Rue Rabelais, which is the finest house in the town and which the town council tried on numerous occasions to list as a historic building. You'll see it.'

'Is Hubert Vernoux still an estate agent?'

'He has a lot of financial commitments. Lucile, his wife's elder sister, lives with them. His son, Alain, the doctor, whom you just met, refuses to practise and is engaged in research that doesn't earn him anything.'

'Married?'

'He married a young lady from Cadeuil, a proper aristocrat, who has already given him three children. The youngest is eight months.'

'Do they live with the father?'

'The house is big enough, as you'll see. That's not all. As well as Alain, Hubert has a daughter, Adeline, who married a certain Paillet, after a holiday romance in Royan. I don't know what he does for a living, but I believe it's Vernoux who provides for them. They spend most of their time in Paris. They put in the occasional appearance for a few days or weeks and I presume that means they're broke. Do you get the picture now?'

'What picture?'

Chabot gave a glum smile which briefly reminded Maigret of his friend of the old days.

'It's true. I'm talking to you as if you were from here. You've seen Vernoux. He is more the country squire than all the local squires. As for his wife and her sister, they seem to vie with each other to make themselves as hateful as possible to the hoi polloi. All that constitutes a clan.'

'And this clan only socializes with a small number of people.'

Chabot turned red for the second time that evening.

'Inevitably,' he muttered, as if guilty.

'So the Vernoux, the Courçons and their friends are a world unto themselves in this town.'

'You've guessed it. Because of my position, I have to see them. And actually, they're not as dreadful as they seem. Take Hubert Vernoux, for instance, I'd swear he's overburdened with worries. He was once very well-off. These days he is less so and I even wonder if he is wealthy at all, because since most of the farmers have become landowners, selling land isn't what it used to be. Hubert is crushed by responsibilities and has a duty to provide for all his relatives. As for Alain, whom I know better, he is a man obsessed.'

'By what?'

'It's best that you know. You will also understand why, earlier, in the street, he and I exchanged worried glances. I told you that Hubert Vernoux's father died from *delirium tremens*. On his wife's side – that is, the Courçons – the history is no better. Old Courçon committed suicide in rather mysterious circumstances that have been hushed up. Hubert had a brother, Basile, whose name is never mentioned, who killed himself at the age of seventeen. Apparently, as far back as you care to go, you'll find insanity or cranks in the family.'

Maigret listened, lazily puffing on his pipe, occasionally taking a sip of brandy.

'That's why Alain studied medicine and chose to work at Sainte-Anne as a junior doctor. It is said, and it's plausible, that most doctors specialize in the diseases to which they think they're susceptible.'

'Alain is haunted by the idea that he belongs to a family of lunatics. According to him, Lucile, his aunt, is half-mad. He hasn't told me, but I'm convinced he spies, not only on his father and mother, but also on his own children.'

'Was this common knowledge?'

'Some talk about it. In small towns, people always gossip and are wary of those who are a bit different from everyone else.'

'Was it mentioned after the first murder in particular?'

Chabot hesitated for a second and nodded.

'Why?'

'Because people knew, or thought they knew, that Hubert Vernoux and his brother-in-law Courçon didn't get on. Perhaps too because they lived right opposite one another.'

'Did they see each other?'

Chabot gave a reluctant little laugh.

'I wonder what you're going to think of us. I have the feeling you don't come across situations like this in Paris.'

In other words, the investigating magistrate was ashamed of a world that was his, in a way, because he lived in it all year round.

'I told you that the Courçons were penniless when Isabelle married Hubert Vernoux. It was Hubert who gave his brother-in-law Robert an allowance. And Robert never forgave him for it. When he spoke of him, he'd say sarcastically: "My brother-in-law the millionaire", or: "I'll go and ask old moneybags." He never set foot inside the big house in Rue Rabelais, whose every coming and going he could see. He lived across the road, in a smaller but very nice house, and had a cleaning woman come every morning. He polished his shoes and cooked his meals himself, made a show of going to the market got up like a landowner inspecting his estate, and brandished a bunch of leeks or asparagus as if it were a trophy. He must have thought that he incensed Hubert.'

'And was Hubert incensed?'

'I don't know. It's possible. But he still continued to provide for his brother-in-law. Several times we saw them exchange acrimonious words when they bumped into one another in the street. One detail you couldn't make up: Robert de Courçon never drew his curtains, so the family opposite watched him going about his life all day long. Some say he'd sometimes poke his tongue out at them.

'But from that to accusing Vernoux of getting rid of him, or of hitting him over the head in a moment of anger . . .'

'Is this what people thought?'

'Yes.'

'Did you think so too?'

'Professionally, at the outset I don't rule out any hypothesis.'

Maigret couldn't help smiling at his pompous words.

'Have you questioned Vernoux?'

'I didn't summon him to my office, if that's what you mean. There wasn't enough evidence to point to a man like him.'

He had said: 'a man like him'.

And Chabot realized that he'd given himself away, that he'd admitted he was more or less part of the clique. Maigret's visit that evening must have been torture for him. It wasn't a pleasure for Maigret either, even though right now he was no longer in such a hurry to leave.

'I saw him in the street, as I do every morning, and asked him a few casual questions.'

'What did he say?'

'That he hadn't left his apartment that evening.'

'What time was the murder committed?'

'The first? Around the same time as today, at approximately ten p.m.'

'What are the Vernoux usually doing at that hour?'

'Apart from bridge on Saturday, which sees the entire family gathered in the sitting room, they all live separate lives without taking any notice of the others.'

'Vernoux doesn't share a bedroom with his wife?'

'He would consider that petty bourgeois. They each have their own apartment, on different floors. Isabelle is on the first floor, and Hubert occupies the ground-floor wing that overlooks the courtyard. Alain's household is on the second floor, and the aunt, Lucile, has two garret rooms on the third. When the daughter and her husband are there . . .'

'Are they here now?'

'No. They're expected in a few days' time.'

'How many servants?'

'A couple, who have been with them for twenty or thirty years, plus two fairly young maids.'

'Where do they sleep?'

'In the other downstairs wing. You'll see the house. It's almost a castle.'

'With a back entrance?'

'There's a door in the courtyard wall, which opens into an alley.'

'So anyone can enter or leave unseen!'

'Probably.'

'You didn't check?'

This was excruciating for Chabot and, because he felt he was in the wrong, he raised his voice, growing almost furious.

'You sound like some of the locals. If I'd gone and questioned the servants when I had no evidence, not the slightest clue, the entire town would have been convinced that either Hubert Vernoux or his son was guilty.'

'His son?'

'Him too, absolutely! Because, given that he doesn't work and dabbles in psychiatry, there are some who think he's mad. He's not a regular at the two cafés, doesn't play snooker or belote, and doesn't chase girls. He will sometimes stop in the street and stare at someone through his glasses which magnify his eyes. He's loathed enough for—'

'Are you defending him?'

'No. I want to keep a cool head and that's not always easy in a small town. I try to be fair. I too thought the first murder was perhaps a family matter. I examined the question from every angle. I was puzzled by the fact that there was no theft and that Robert de Courçon didn't put up a struggle. And I would probably have taken certain steps if—'

'Just a second. You didn't ask the police to follow Hubert Vernoux and his son?'

'You can do that in Paris, but not here. Everyone knows our four poor police officers. As for the Poitiers inspectors, people spotted them before they had even got out of their car! It is rare to find more than ten people in the street at any one time. And you want to follow someone under these conditions without their noticing?'

Abruptly, he calmed down.

'I'm sorry. I'm talking so loudly that I'll wake my mother. It's just that I wanted to make you understand my position. Until there's evidence to the contrary, the Vernoux are innocent. I'd swear they are. The second murder, two days after the first, was almost the proof. Hubert Vernoux might have been driven to kill his brother-in-law, to hit him in a moment of anger. But he had no reason to go off to the end of Rue des Loges and slaughter the widow Gibon, whom he probably doesn't even know.'

'Who is she?'

'A former midwife whose long-dead husband was a police officer. She lived alone, half-crippled, in a three-roomed house.

'Not only is there the old Gibon woman, but, tonight, Gobillard. Now, the Vernoux did know him, as did the whole of Fontenay. In every French town, there's at least one drunkard like him who's a sort of local character.

'If you can give me one single reason to kill a man like that . . .'

'Supposing he saw something?'

'What about the widow Gibon, who never left her house? Might she have seen something too? Might she have come to Rue Rabelais after ten o'clock at night, and witnessed the murder through the window? No, you see. I know all about crime investigation methods. I didn't attend the Bordeaux congress and I may not be au fait with the latest scientific discoveries, but I believe I know my job and carry it out conscientiously. The three victims were from completely different social milieus and there is no connection between them. All three were killed in the same way, and, from the wounds, it would seem with the same weapon. All three were attacked from the front, which suggests their suspicions weren't aroused. If it is a madman, it's not one who waves his arms around or raves, which would have made them get out of his way. So it's what I'd call a lucid madman, who follows a particular behaviour pattern and is astute enough to take precautions.'

'Alain Vernoux didn't give much of an explanation as to why he was out in the pouring rain this evening.'

'He said he was going to see a friend on the other side of the Champ-de-Mars.'

'He didn't give a name.'

'Because there's no need. I know he often visits a certain Georges Vassal, who's a bachelor and an old school friend. Even without that detail, I wouldn't have been surprised.'

'Why not?'

'Because he's even more interested in the case than I am, for personal reasons. I wouldn't venture to say that he suspects his father, but I'm tempted. A few weeks ago he talked to me about him and the family flaws—'

'Just like that, out of the blue?'

'No. He'd come back from La Roche-sur-Yon and was telling me about a case he'd studied. That of a man in his early sixties who had always behaved normally, but suddenly became insane the day he had to pay the dowry he'd promised his daughter. People didn't notice right away.'

'In other words, you think Alain Vernoux wandered around Fontenay during the night in search of the murderer?'

The investigating magistrate grew indignant again.

'I would think he's better qualified to recognize a madman in the street than our valiant police officers who are combing the town, or than you or I.'

Maigret said nothing.

It was gone midnight.

'Are you sure you don't want to stay here?'

'My luggage is at the hotel.'

'Will I see you tomorrow morning?'

'Of course.'

'I'll be at the law courts. You know where they are?'

'Rue Rabelais, aren't they?'

'A bit higher up than the Vernoux's house. First of all you'll see the prison gates, then a rather ugly building. My office is at the end of the corridor, near the prosecutor's.'

'Good night, old friend.'

'I haven't been a very good host.'

'Don't be ridiculous!'

'You must understand my frame of mind. It's the kind of case that can turn the entire town against me.'

'Of course!'

'Are you making fun of me?'

'I assure you I'm not.'

And he wasn't. Rather, Maigret felt a kind of sadness, as he always did when a little of the past evaporated. In the hall, as he put on his sodden overcoat, he inhaled the smell of the house, which he had always found so fragrant, but which now seemed stale to him.

Chabot had lost most of his hair and his balding head was pointed like that of some birds.

'I'll walk you back . . .'

He didn't want to. He was merely being polite.

'Not on your life!'

Maigret joked rather pathetically, in order to say something and leave on a cheerful note:

'I can swim!'

After which, turning up his coat collar, he stepped out into the squall. Julien Chabot stood on the doorstep for a while, in the rectangle of jaundiced light, then closed the door behind him and Maigret had the feeling that he was the only person out and about.

3. *The School Teacher Who Never Slept*

The streets looked more depressing in the daylight than at night because the rain had dirtied everything, leaving dark trails on the façades, whose colours had become unsightly. Huge drops were still splashing from the cornices and the electricity cables, and sometimes from the dripping sky, which was still menacing and seemed to be gathering strength for a fresh onslaught.

Maigret, having risen late, hadn't had the heart to go downstairs for breakfast. Grumpy, with no appetite, all he wanted was two or three cups of black coffee. Despite Chabot's brandy, he thought he still had in his mouth the aftertaste of the overly sweet white wine he had drunk in Bordeaux.

He pressed a little bell dangling by the bed. The chambermaid in a black dress and white apron who answered his call gave him such a strange look that he checked that he was decently dressed.

'Do you really not want any warm croissants? A man like you needs to eat in the morning.'

'Just coffee, my dear. A big pot of coffee.'

She spotted the suit that Maigret had hung up to dry over the radiator and grabbed it.

'What are you doing?'

'I'm going to give it an iron.'

'No, thank you, there's no point.'

She took it away regardless.

From her appearance, he would have sworn that she was usually on the surly side.

Twice, while he was washing and dressing, she came and disturbed him, once to make sure he had some soap, and then to bring him another pot of coffee that he hadn't requested. Then she brought back the suit, dried and ironed. She was thin and flat-chested, with a rather sickly look to her, but was probably as tough as nails.

He reckoned she must have seen his name downstairs on the registration card and was an avid reader of the crime pages.

It was 9.30. He lazed around in protest against he didn't know what, against what he vaguely felt to be a conspiracy of fate.

As he descended the red-carpeted stairs, a handyman who was on his way up greeted him with a respectful:

'Good morning, Monsieur Maigret.'

It all made sense when he reached the lobby, where he found the *Ouest-Éclair* with his photo on the front page spread on a pedestal table.

It was the photo taken when he had been leaning over Gobillard's body. A double headline screamed over three columns:

INSPECTOR MAIGRET INVESTIGATES THE FONTENAY MURDERS

RABBIT-FUR SELLER IS THIRD VICTIM

Before he'd had the time to skim through the article, the hotel manager was rushing towards him as eagerly as the chambermaid.

'I hope you slept well and that number seventeen didn't disturb you?'

'What's number seventeen?'

'A travelling salesman who had too much to drink last night and made a lot of noise. We moved him to another room so he wouldn't wake you.'

Maigret hadn't heard a thing.

'By the way, Lomel, the reporter from the *Ouest-Éclair*, came by this morning to see you. When I told him you were still in bed, he said it wasn't urgent and that he'd catch you later at the law courts. There's also a letter for you.'

A cheap envelope, the sort that are sold in general stores in packets of six, all different colours. This one was a greenish hue. As he opened it, Maigret noticed that outside half a dozen people had their faces pressed to the glass door, between the potted palm trees.

Dont be dicieved by them rich folk.

The people waiting on the pavement, including two women dressed as market stallholders, stood aside to let him through and there was something trusting, friendly, in the way they gazed at him – not so much out of curiosity or because he was famous, but as if they were counting on him. One of the women said, without daring to venture closer:

'You'll find him, you will, Monsieur Maigret!'

And a young man who looked like a delivery boy kept pace with him on the other side of the road so as to get a better look at him.

Women standing on their doorsteps discussing the latest murder broke off to gaze after him. A group came out of the Café de la Poste and, in their eyes too, he read friendliness. People seemed to want to encourage him.

He walked past Chabot's house, where Rose was shaking dust-cloths out of the first-floor window, and didn't stop but crossed Place Viète and continued up Rue Rabelais where, to his left, rose a huge mansion with a coat of arms on the pediment which must have been the Vernoux family home. There was no sign of life behind the closed windows. Opposite, a little house with fastened shutters, also old, was probably the one where Robert de Courçon's solitary life had ended.

There was an occasional gust of dank wind. Low, dark clouds rolled across a sky the colour of frosted glass, and drops of water fell from their edges. The wetness made the prison gates look even blacker. A dozen people were assembled outside the law courts, which were quite unimpressive, being less vast, in fact, than the Vernoux's residence, albeit adorned with a peristyle and a flight of steps.

Lomel, two cameras still slung over his shoulder, was the first to hurry over, and there wasn't a trace of remorse on his chubby face or in his very light blue eyes.

'Will you tell me your impressions before you talk to my fellow journalists from Paris?'

And, because Maigret, disgruntled, was pointing at the newspaper poking out of his pocket, he smiled.

'Are you angry?'

'I thought I told you—'

'Look, inspector. I have to do my job as a reporter. I knew you'd end up in charge of the case. I simply anticipated by a few hours.'

'Next time, don't anticipate.'

'Are you going to see Chabot?'

There were already two or three reporters from Paris among the group, and he had trouble shaking them off. There were also curious bystanders who seemed determined to spend the day watching the law courts.

The corridors were gloomy. Lomel, who had appointed himself Maigret's guide, walked ahead of him and showed him the way.

'Follow me. It's much more important for us than for the Paris papers! You must understand! "He" has been in his office since eight o'clock this morning. The prosecutor's here too. Last night, they were looking for him everywhere, but he'd driven over to La Rochelle. Do you know the prosecutor?'

Maigret, who had knocked and been bidden to enter, opened the door and closed it behind him, leaving the ginger-haired reporter in the corridor.

Julien Chabot wasn't alone. Doctor Alain Vernoux was sitting facing him in an armchair, and he rose to greet Maigret.

'Slept well?' asked the magistrate.

'Not at all badly.'

'I was annoyed with myself for my poor hospitality yesterday. You know Alain Vernoux. He dropped in to see me in passing.'

It wasn't true. Maigret would have sworn that the psychiatrist was waiting for him and even, perhaps, that this meeting had been contrived by the two men.

Alain had removed his overcoat. He was wearing a crumpled coarse-wool suit that could have done with an iron. His tie was clumsily knotted. A yellow sweater poked out below his jacket. His shoes hadn't been polished. Even like this, he still belonged to the same class as his father whose dress was so meticulous.

Why did that make Maigret frown? One was too immaculate, all spruced up. The other, by contrast, affected a carelessness that a bank clerk, schoolmaster or a travelling salesman would not have permitted himself, but suits in that fabric could probably only be made by a bespoke tailor in Paris, or perhaps Bordeaux.

There was a rather awkward silence. Maigret, who did nothing to help the two men, planted himself in front of the meagre log fire. On the mantelpiece stood the same black marble clock as the one in his office at Quai des Orfèvres. The police department must once have ordered them by the hundred if not the thousand. Maybe they were all twelve minutes slow, like Maigret's?

'Alain was just telling me some interesting things,' Chabot muttered at length, his chin in his hand, in an attitude that made him look very much the investigating magistrate.

'We were talking about criminal insanity—'

Alain Vernoux broke in:

'I didn't say that these three murders are the work of a madman. I said that *if they were the work of a madman . . .*'

'It boils down to the same thing.'

'Not exactly.'

'Let us assume I was the one who said that everything seems to suggest we are dealing with a madman.'

And, turning to Maigret:

'We talked about this last night, you and I. The absence of a motive, in all three cases . . . The same method . . .'

Then, to Vernoux:

'Tell the detective chief inspector what you were explaining to me, would you?'

'I'm no expert on the subject, but merely an amateur. I was expanding on a general idea. Most people think the insane always act as if they are insane, in other words illogically and irrationally. But as a matter of fact, it is often the contrary. The insane have their own logic. The challenge is to find out what that logic is.'

Maigret looked at him with his big, slightly bleary morning eyes, but said nothing. He regretted not having stopped on the way for a drink that would have perked him up.

The cramped office, where the smoke from his pipe was creating a haze and the short flames from the logs were dancing, seemed almost unreal to him, and the two men discussing insanity and watching him out of the corner of their eyes looked like waxworks. They weren't for real either. They made gestures that they had been taught, spoke as they had been taught to speak.

What could a Chabot know about what happened in the street? And, more to the point, inside the head of a man who kills?

'It is that logic that I've been trying to fathom since the first murder.'

'Since the first murder?'

'Well, since the second. From the start, though, from when my uncle was killed, I thought it might be the act of a madman.'

'And have you fathomed it out?'

'Not yet. I've identified only a few elements of the problem, which might provide some clue.'

'For instance?'

'For instance, that *he* strikes from the front. It's hard for me to put this simply. A man who wants to kill for the sake of killing, in other words to eliminate other living beings, but at the same time, doesn't want to get caught, would choose the least risky means. But this one certainly doesn't want to get caught, because he makes sure to leave no evidence. Are you with me?'

'So far it's not very difficult.'

Vernoux frowned, sensing the sarcasm in Maigret's tone. It was possible, in fact, that he was shy. He didn't look people in the eyes. Hiding behind his thick spectacle lenses, he contented himself with furtive little glances, then stared at a point somewhere in space.

'Would you say that he goes to great lengths to avoid being caught?'

'Apparently.'

'All the same, he attacks three people in one week and all three times he succeeds.'

'Exactly.'

'In all three cases, he could have struck from behind, which would have reduced the chances of one of his victims starting to scream.'

Maigret stared at him.

'Since even a madman doesn't do anything for no reason, I infer that the murderer feels the need to taunt fate, or taunt his victims. Some people need to assert themselves, either through a crime or through a series of crimes. Sometimes it's to prove their power or their importance or their bravery to themselves. Others are convinced that they need to avenge themselves against their fellow creatures.'

His chin still resting on his hands, Chabot broke in, sounding pleased with himself.

'So far, this murderer has only attacked the weak. Robert de Courçon was an old man of seventy-three. The widow Gibon was an invalid and Gobillard was blind drunk when he was attacked.'

'That occurred to me too. Perhaps it's a sign, perhaps a coincidence. What I'm trying to find is the logic governing the unknown murderer's comings and goings. When we have found that out, we will be close to nabbing him.'

Vernoux said 'we' as if he were naturally part of the investigation, and Chabot raised no objection.

'Is that why you were out in the streets last night?' asked Maigret.

Alain Vernoux gave a start and reddened a little.

'Partly. I was going to see a friend, but I confess that for the past three days I've been combing the streets as often as possible to study the behaviour of the passers-by. This isn't a very big town. It is likely that the murderer isn't staying locked up indoors. He's out and about like everyone else, perhaps having a drink in a café.'

'Do you think you'd spot him if you met him?'

'It's possible.'

'I believe Alain can be a great help to us,' murmured Chabot with a certain awkwardness. 'What he's said to us this morning makes a lot of sense.'

The doctor rose and, at the same time, there was a noise in the corridor and a knock on the door. Inspector Chabiron poked his head around the door.

'You're not alone?' he said, looking not at Maigret, but at Alain Vernoux, whose presence appeared to irk him.

'What is it, inspector?'

'I have someone here whom I'd like you to question.'

The doctor announced:

'I'll be off.'

No one stopped him. As he was leaving, Chabiron said to Maigret, not without resentment:

'So, chief, looks like you're handling things?'

'So it says in the papers.'

'Perhaps the investigation won't last long. It could be over in a few minutes. Shall I bring in my witness, sir?'

And, turning towards the dimly lit corridor:

'Come in! Don't be afraid.'

A voice replied:

'I'm not afraid.'

A short, skinny man entered, dressed in navy blue, with a pale face and fiery eyes.

Chabiron introduced him:

'Émile Chalus, teacher at the boys' school. Sit down, Chalus.'

Chabiron was one of those police officers who treated offenders and witnesses with familiarity, convinced that it intimidated them.

'Last night,' he explained, 'I started questioning the people who live in the street where Gobillard was killed. Some might say it was routine . . .'

He shot a look at Maigret, as if he were a personal enemy of routine.

' . . . but sometimes routine is useful. It's not a long street. This morning, early, I continued going over it with a fine-tooth comb. Émile Chalus lives thirty metres from the spot where the murder was committed, on the second floor of a house whose ground and first floor are offices. Tell them, Chalus.'

Chalus didn't need asking twice, although he clearly had no liking for the investigating magistrate. He turned towards Maigret.

'I heard a noise on the pavement, like the stamping of feet.'

'What time was that?'

'Just after ten o'clock at night.'

'And then?'

'Footsteps fading.'

'In which direction?'

The investigating magistrate asked the questions, glancing at Maigret each time as if inviting him to speak.

'In the direction of Rue de la République.'

'Hurried steps?'

'No, normal steps.'

'A man's?'

'Definitely.'

Chabot appeared to think that this was no great revelation, but the inspector interrupted:

'Wait till you hear the rest. Tell them what happened next, Chalus.'

'Some minutes went by and a group of people entered the street, coming from Rue de la République too. They gathered on the pavement, talking loudly. I heard the word "doctor", then "detective inspector", and I got up to go and look out of the window.'

Chabiron was jubilant.

'You see, sir? Chalus heard the stamping of feet. Earlier, he told me that there was also a thud, like that of a body falling on to the pavement. Tell them what you told me, Chalus.'

'That's correct.'

'Immediately afterwards, someone headed towards Rue de la République, where the Café de la Poste is. I have other witnesses in the waiting room, customers who were in the café at that time. It was ten past ten when Doctor Vernoux came in and made straight for the telephone booth, without saying anything. After making a call, he spotted Doctor Jussieux playing cards and whispered something in his ear. Jussieux announced to the others that a murder had just been committed and they all raced outside.'

Maigret stared at his friend Chabot, whose expression was frozen.

'Do you see what that means?' the inspector went on with a sort of aggressive relish, as if he were exacting a personal revenge.

'According to Doctor Vernoux, he saw a body lying on the pavement, a body already almost cold, and he went into the Café de la Poste to telephone the police. If that were the case, there would have been two sets of footsteps in the street and Chalus, who wasn't asleep, would have heard them.'

He didn't dare crow yet, but his mounting excitement was palpable.

'Chalus doesn't have a police record. He's a respected teacher. He has no reason to make up such a story.'

Again Maigret ignored his friend's unspoken invitation to say something. A fairly lengthy silence ensued. Probably to keep up appearances, the magistrate scribbled a few words in the file he had in front of him and, when he looked up, he was tense.

'Are you married, Monsieur Chalus?' he asked in a dull voice.

'Yes, sir.'

The hostility between the two men was tangible. Chalus too was tense, and his replies were aggressive. He seemed to be challenging the magistrate to reject his statement.

'Children?'

'No.'

'Was your wife with you last night?'

'In the same bed.'

'Was she asleep?'

'Yes.'

'Did you go to bed at the same time?'

'As usual when I don't have too much homework to mark. Yesterday was Friday and I didn't have any at all.'

'What time did you turn in with your wife?'

'At half past nine, perhaps a few minutes later.'

'Do you always go to sleep so early?'

'We get up at half past five in the morning.'

'Why?'

'Because we take advantage of the freedom enjoyed by all French citizens to get up when they choose.'

Maigret, who was watching him with interest, would have sworn that he was involved in politics, belonged to a left-wing party and was probably what was known as an activist. He was the sort of man to go on marches, address meetings, and also the sort of man to slip pamphlets through letterboxes and refuse to move on when told to do so by the police.

'So you both went to bed at half past nine and I presume you fell asleep?'

'We chatted for around ten minutes.'

'That takes us to nine forty. Did you both doze off?'

'My wife fell asleep.'

'What about you?'

'No. I find it hard to get to sleep.'

'So that when you heard a noise on the pavement, thirty metres from your house, you weren't asleep?'

'That's correct.'

'Had you not slept at all?'

'No.'

'Were you fully awake?'

'Enough to hear stamping of feet and the thud of a body falling.'

'Was it raining?'

'Yes.'

'There's no floor above you?'

'No. We're on the second floor.'

'You must have heard the rain on the roof?'

'After a while you take no notice any more.'

'The water in the guttering?'

'Definitely.'

'So the noises you heard were merely sounds among various others?'

'There's a clear difference between running water and the stamping of feet or the sound of a body falling.'

The magistrate still would not let up:

'Weren't you curious enough to get out of bed?'

'No.'

'Why not?'

'Because we're not far from the Café de la Poste.'

'I don't understand.'

'At night, it often happens that people who've had too much to drink go past our house, and they sometimes fall flat on their faces in the street.'

'And remain lying there?'

Chalus had no immediate answer.

'Since you mentioned the stamping of feet, I presume you had the impression that there were several men in the street, or at least two?'

'That goes without saying.'

'Only one man ran off in the direction of Rue de la République. Is that right?'

'I suppose so.'

'Given that a murder took place, two men at least were thirty metres from your house at the time you caught that sound. Do you follow me?'

'It's not difficult.'

'And you heard one of them leaving?'

'I already said so.'

'When did you hear them arrive? Did they arrive together? Did they come from Rue de la République or from the Champ-de-Mars?'

Chabiron shrugged, while Émile Chalus racked his brains, his expression steely.

'I didn't hear them arrive.'

'You don't really think that, do you, that they had been standing in the rain for long, one waiting for the right moment to kill the other?'

The school teacher clenched his fists.

'Is that all you can come up with?' he muttered under his breath.

'I don't understand.'

'It annoys you that someone from your world is under suspicion. But your question doesn't make sense. I don't necessarily hear someone walking past in the street, or to be more precise, I don't take any notice.'

'And yet . . .'

'Let me finish, will you, instead of trying to trip me up. Until the moment when I heard the stamping of feet, I had no reason to take any notice of what was going on in the street. After that, on the contrary, my mind was on the alert.'

'And you contend that from the moment when the body fell on the pavement until the moment when several people came running from the Café de la Poste, no one walked down the street?'

'There were no footsteps.'

'Are you aware of the importance of that assertion?'

'I didn't ask to make it. It is the inspector who came to question me.'

'Before the inspector questioned you, did you have any idea of the importance of your testimony?'

'I was unaware of Doctor Vernoux's statement.'

'Who said anything about a statement? Doctor Vernoux has not been called upon to make a statement.'

'Let's say I was unaware of his version of events.'

'Was it the inspector who told you about it?'

'Yes.'

'Did you understand?'

'Yes.'

'And I imagine you were delighted at the effect you were going to produce? You hate the Vernoux family, don't you?'

'Them and all those of their kind.'

'And you have singled them out for attack in your speeches?'

'I have done.'

The magistrate, frosty, turned to Inspector Chabiron:

'Has his wife confirmed his story?'

'Partially. I didn't bring her in because she was busy with her housework, but I can go and fetch her. They did go to bed at nine thirty. She's certain of it because she's the one who wound up the alarm-clock, as usual. They chatted for a bit. She fell asleep and what woke her was not feeling her husband beside her. She saw him standing at the window. That was at ten fifteen, and at that point a group of people were gathered around the body.'

'And neither of them went down?'

'No.'

'They weren't curious to find out what was going on?'

'They opened the window a little and heard that Gobillard had just been knocked out.'

Chabot, who was still avoiding Maigret's eye, seemed disheartened. He asked a few more questions, without conviction:

'Have other residents in the street confirmed his story?'

'Not so far.'

'Have you questioned them all?'

'The ones who were at home this morning. Some had already left for work. Two or three others were at the cinema last night and know nothing.'

Chabot turned to the school teacher.

'Do you know Doctor Vernoux personally?'

'I've never spoken to him, if that's what you mean. I've often walked past him in the street, like everyone else. I know who he is.'

'You have no particular animosity towards him?'

'I've already answered you.'

'Have you ever appeared in court?'

'I've been arrested at least a dozen times, during political demonstrations, but I've always been released after one night in the lock-up and, of course, a beating.'

'That's not what I'm talking about.'

'I see that doesn't interest you.'

'Do you stand by your statement?'

'Yes, even if you don't like it.'

'This isn't about me.'

'It's about your friends.'

'You are certain enough of what you heard last night to have no hesitation in sending someone to prison or to the gallows?'

'I'm not the one who killed. The murderer had no hesitation, did he, in killing the widow Gibon and poor Gobillard.'

'You're forgetting Robert de Courçon.'

'I couldn't care less about him!'

'I'm going to call the clerk so he can take down your statement.'

'Whenever it suits you.'

'Then we'll speak to your wife.'

'She won't contradict me.'

Chabot was already reaching for an electric buzzer on his desk when Maigret, whose presence they had almost forgotten, asked quietly:

'Do you suffer from insomnia, Monsieur Chalus?'

The latter turned his head abruptly.

'What are you trying to insinuate?'

'Nothing. I thought I heard you say earlier that you found it hard to get to sleep, which explains why you were still awake at ten o'clock, having gone to bed at half past nine.'

'I've suffered from insomnia for years.'

'Have you seen the doctor?'

'I don't like doctors.'

'You haven't tried any remedies?'

'I take pills.'

'Every day?'

'Is that a crime?'

'Did you take one last night, before going to bed?'

'I took two, as usual.'

Maigret nearly smiled on seeing his friend Chabot come back to life like a thirsty plant that is watered at last. The magistrate couldn't help taking charge of operations again himself.

'Why didn't you tell us that you had taken sleeping tablets?'

'Because you didn't ask me and it's my business. Am I supposed to tell you when my wife takes a laxative as well?'

'You took two tablets at half past nine?'

'Yes.'

'And you weren't asleep at ten past ten?'

'No. If you were familiar with those drugs, you'd know that after a while they have almost no effect any more. At first, one tablet was enough. Now, with two, it takes me more than half an hour to drop off.'

'So it's possible that when you heard the noise in the street you had already fallen asleep?'

'I wasn't asleep. If I'd been asleep, I wouldn't have heard anything.'

'But you could have been dozing. What were you thinking about?'

'I don't remember.'

'Do you swear that you weren't half-asleep and half-awake? Consider my question carefully. Perjury is a serious offence.'

'I was not asleep.'

The man was honest, deep down. There was no doubt he had been thrilled to be able to bring down a member of the Vernoux clan and he had done so with relish. Now, feeling his triumph slip through his fingers, he was trying to cling on, without daring to go so far as to lie.

He shot Maigret a sad look that contained reproach but not anger. He seemed to be saying: 'Why did you betray me, when you're not on their side?'

Chabot wasted no time.

'Supposing the pills had begun to take effect, without sending you completely to sleep, it is possible that you could have heard sounds in the street and your drowsiness would explain the fact that you didn't hear the sound of footsteps before the murder. It took the stamping of feet, the thud of the body falling, to attract your attention. Is it not conceivable that afterwards, once the footsteps died away, you fell asleep again? You didn't get out of bed. You didn't waken your wife. You weren't unduly concerned, you told us, as if it had all happened in a dream. It was only when a group of men down in the street were talking in loud voices that you fully woke up.'

Chalus gave a weary shrug.

'I should have expected this,' he said.

Then he added something like:

'You and your sort . . .'

Chabot wasn't listening any more. He was saying to Inspector Chabiron:

'Take down his statement anyway. I'll question his wife this afternoon.'

When he and Maigret were alone, the magistrate put on a show of making notes. Five minutes went by before he muttered, without looking at Maigret:

'Thank you.'

And, puffing on his pipe, Maigret replied gruffly:

'You're welcome.'

4. *The Italian Woman with Bruises*

Throughout the entire lunch, whose main course was a stuffed shoulder of lamb the likes of which Maigret couldn't remember ever having eaten, Julien Chabot seemed like a man suffering from a guilty conscience.

As they entered the house, he had felt the need to murmur:

'Let's not talk of this in front of my mother.'

Maigret had no intention of doing so. He saw his friend bend over the letterbox and, pushing aside various leaflets, pick up an envelope similar to the one that had been handed to him that morning at the hotel. But this one, instead of being a greenish colour, was salmon pink. Perhaps it came from the same writing set? He couldn't check because the magistrate slipped it casually into his pocket.

They had hardly spoken on the way back from the law courts. Before leaving, they had had a brief conversation with the prosecutor and Maigret had been quite surprised to find that he was a man of barely thirty, fresh out of law school, a handsome fellow who did not seem overly burdened by his duties.

'Apologies for last night, Chabot. There's a good reason why no one could get hold of me. I was in La Rochelle without my wife's knowledge.'

He added with a wink:

'Luckily!'

Then, not suspecting a thing:

'Now that you have Detective Chief Inspector Maigret to help you, it won't take you long to catch the murderer. Do you also think it's a madman, sir?'

What was the point of arguing? It was clear that relations between the magistrate and the prosecutor weren't exactly friendly.

In the corridor, they were besieged by journalists already informed of Chalus' statement. He must have talked to them. Maigret was convinced that, in town too, people knew. It was hard to explain that particular atmosphere. On the way from the law courts to the magistrate's house, they came across no more than around fifty souls, but that was enough to gauge the local mood. The two men read mistrust in their eyes. The common folk, especially the women on their way back from the market, had an almost hostile attitude. At the top of Place Viète there was a little café where a number of people were having an aperitif and, as they walked past, they heard an unfriendly murmur and sniggers.

Some must have been starting to feel alarmed, and the presence of the gendarmes patrolling the streets on bicycles was not enough to reassure them; on the contrary, they added a note of drama, a reminder that there was a killer at large.

Madame Chabot hadn't attempted to ask any questions. She fussed over her son, over Maigret too, seeming to be imploring him with her eyes to protect Julien, and she tried hard to bring up agreeable subjects of conversation.

'Do you remember that girl with a squint whom you met at dinner here one Sunday?'

She had a terrifying memory, reminding Maigret of aquaintances he had encountered some thirty years earlier, during his brief stays in Fontenay.

'She made a good marriage; a young man from Marans who founded a large dairy. They had three children, each more beautiful than the other, then suddenly, as if fate thought they were too happy, she contracted tuberculosis.'

She spoke of others, who had fallen ill or died, or suffered misfortunes.

For dessert, Rose brought in a huge dish of profiteroles and the old woman watched Maigret with a mischievous look in her eyes. At first he wondered why, sensing that something was expected of him. He wasn't very fond of profiteroles, but he took one.

'Go on! Help yourself. Don't be shy!'

Seeing her disappointment, he took three.

'You're not going to tell me you've lost your appetite? I remember that evening when you ate twelve. Each time you came, I made you profiteroles and you declared you had never eaten such delicious ones anywhere.'

(Which, incidentally, was true: he never ate profiteroles anywhere else!)

He had no recollection of it. He was even surprised that he had ever expressed a liking for pastries. He must have said that, in the past, to be polite.

He did what was expected, exclaimed with pleasure, ate everything that was on his plate, and helped himself to more.

'And the partridge with cabbage! Do you remember? I'm sorry it's not the season, because . . .'

Coffee was served and she tactfully withdrew. Out of habit, Chabot placed a box of cigars on the table along with the bottle of brandy. The dining room had no more changed than the study and it was almost painful to find everything exactly as it had been. Even Chabot, seen in a certain way, appeared unchanged.

Maigret helped himself to a cigar to please his friend and stretched out his legs in front of the hearth. He knew that Chabot wanted to raise a particular matter, that he had been preoccupied since they had left the courts. It took him a while. The voice of the magistrate, who was looking elsewhere, was lacking in confidence.

'Do you think I should have arrested him?'

'Who?'

'Alain.'

'I don't see any reason to arrest the doctor.'

'Chalus seems to be telling the truth, though.'

'There's no doubt about that.'

'Do you also think he wasn't lying?'

Inwardly, Chabot was wondering why Maigret had stepped in because, had it not been for him, without the question of the sleeping tablets, the teacher's statement would have been much more damning for the younger Vernoux. This intrigued the magistrate and made him uncomfortable.

'First of all,' said Maigret awkwardly smoking his cigar, 'it is possible that he really did drop off. I am always wary of the testimony of people who have heard something when in bed, perhaps because of my wife.

'She frequently claims she has lain awake until two o'clock in the morning. She truly believes it, is prepared to swear to it. But I'm myself often awake during her so-called insomnia, and I've seen her fast asleep.'

Chabot was not convinced. Perhaps he thought to himself that his friend had simply wanted to get him out of a tight spot?

'I would add,' Maigret went on, 'that even if the doctor is the killer, it is better not to have arrested him. He's not a man from whom you can extract a confession with a little light questioning, even less by roughing him up.'

The magistrate was already indignantly brushing away this notion.

'At the present stage of the investigation, there isn't even a shred of evidence against him. In arresting him, you would be pandering to a section of the population that would come and demonstrate outside the prison shouting: "Death to the murderer!" Once the rabble was stirred up, it would be hard to calm them down.'

'Do you really think so?'

'Yes.'

'You're not just saying that to make me feel better?'

'I'm saying it because it's the truth. As always happens in a case like this, public opinion more or less openly points to a suspect, and I have often wondered why. It's a mysterious, rather terrifying phenomenon. If I understand correctly, from day one people's suspicions fell on the Vernoux family, no matter whether it was the father or the son.'

'That's right.'

'Now, the anger is directed at the son.'

'What if he is the murderer?'

'Before leaving, I heard you giving orders to have him shadowed.'

'He can elude the surveillance.'

'That wouldn't be wise on his part, because if he shows his face too much in town, he's likely to get lynched. If it is him, sooner or later he'll do something that will provide a clue.'

'Perhaps you're right. To be honest, I'm glad you're here. Yesterday, I admit, I was a little irritated. I was worried you'd be watching me and that you'd find me awkward, clumsy and old-fashioned. In the provinces we nearly all have an inferiority complex, especially vis-à-vis those who come from Paris. All the more so when it's a man like you! Are you angry with me?'

'About what?'

'About the stupid things I said to you.'

'You talked a lot of sense. In Paris too we have to take situations into account and handle people with kid gloves.'

Chabot felt better already.

'I'm going to spend my afternoon questioning the witnesses Chabiron's unearthed for me. Most of them saw nothing and heard nothing, but I don't want to leave any stone unturned.'

'Be gentle with Chalus' wife.'

'Admit that you have a soft spot for those people.'

'Yes, probably!'

'Will you come with me?'

'No. I prefer to sniff around town and have a beer here and there.'

'By the way, I haven't opened this letter. I didn't want to do so in front of my mother.'

He drew the salmon-pink envelope out of his pocket and Maigret recognized the handwriting. The paper came from the same writing set as the note he had received that morning.

Try and find out what the doctor done to the Sabati gurl.

'Do you know her?'

'Never heard that name.'

'I think I recall your saying that Doctor Vernoux isn't a womanizer.'

'He is reputed not to be. Anonymous letters are going to start pouring in. This one comes from a woman.'

'As do most anonymous letters. Would you mind telephoning the police station?'

'About the Sabati girl?'

'Yes.'

'Right away?'

Maigret nodded.

'Let's go into my study.'

He picked up the receiver and dialled.

'Is that you, Féron? Investigating magistrate Chabot here. Do you know a woman named Sabati?'

They had to wait. Féron went and asked his officers, perhaps looked through the log books. When he came back to the phone, Chabot scribbled a few words on his blotter as he listened.

'No. Probably no connection . . . What? . . . Certainly not. Don't worry about her for the time being.'

As he said this, his eyes sought Maigret's approval and the latter nodded emphatically.

'I'll be in my office in half an hour . . . Yes . . . Thank you.'

He hung up.

'There's a Louise Sabati in Fontenay-le-Comte. The daughter of an Italian builder who probably works in Nantes or the surrounding area. She was a waitress at the Hôtel de France for a while, and then at the Café de la Poste. She hasn't worked for several months. Unless she's moved recently, she lives in the barracks neighbourhood in lodgings in a large, ramshackle house on the bend on the La Rochelle road where six or seven families live.'

Maigret, who had had enough of his cigar, stubbed out the smouldering tip in the ashtray and then filled a pipe.

'Do you intend to go and see her?'

'Maybe.'

'Do you still think that the doctor —?'

He broke off, frowning.

'By the way, what are we going to do this evening? I would normally be playing bridge at the Vernoux's. From what you told me, Hubert Vernoux is expecting you to come with me.'

'Well?'

'I wonder whether, given the public mood . . .'

'Are you in the habit of going there every Saturday?'

'Yes.'

'So if you don't go, people will conclude that they are under suspicion.'

'And if I go, people will say . . .'

'People will say you're protecting them, that's all. They already are. A little more or a little less . . .'

'Do you plan to come with me?'

'Absolutely.'

'If you want to . . .'

Poor Chabot gave up arguing and went along with Maigret's suggestions.

'It's time for me to go over to the courts.'

They left the house together and the sky was still the same luminous but murky white, like a sky seen reflected in a pond. On the street corners, the strong wind plastered the women's dresses to their bodies; sometimes a man's hat blew off and he would run after it flailing absurdly.

They each set off in separate directions.

'When will I see you again?'

'I may drop into your chambers. Otherwise I'll be at your house for dinner. What time is bridge at the Vernoux's?'

'Half past eight.'

'I must warn you I don't know how to play.'

'That doesn't matter.'

Curtains twitched as Maigret walked past, following the pavement, his pipe between his teeth, his hands in his pockets and his head bowed to stop his hat from flying off. Once alone, he felt a little less sure of himself. Everything he had just said to his friend Chabot was true. But when he had intervened that morning at the end of Chalus' questioning, he had been acting on a hunch as well as wanting to rescue the magistrate from an awkward situation.

The towns people were still jittery. Although they went about their day-to-day activities as usual, there was anxiety in their eyes and they seemed to be walking faster, as if they were afraid the murderer would suddenly appear. Maigret would have sworn the housewives didn't normally stand around on doorsteps talking in hushed tones.

People gazed after him and he thought he could read an unasked question on their faces. Was he going to do something? Or would the stranger be able to carry on killing with impunity?

Some greeted him timidly, as if to say: We know who you are. You have the reputation of solving the most difficult cases. And, *you* won't let yourself be intimidated by a handful of big shots.'

He nearly went into the Café de la Poste to have a beer. Unfortunately, there were at least a dozen customers inside, who all turned to look at him when he approached, and right then he didn't feel like having to alleviate their worries.

To reach the barracks neighbourhood he had to cross the Champ-de-Mars, a vast, bare parade ground surrounded by recently planted trees that trembled in the north wind.

He turned into the same sidestreet that the doctor had taken the previous evening, the one where Gobillard had been attacked. As he walked past a house, he heard the sound of raised voices coming from the second floor. That was probably the home of Émile Chalus, the teacher. Several people were arguing hotly, friends of his who must have come over to find out what was going on.

He crossed the Champ-de-Mars, skirted the barracks and headed down the street off to the right, looking for the big run-down building his friend had described. There was only one that fitted the description, in an empty street between two patches of wasteland. It was hard to guess what it might have been in the past – a warehouse or a mill, perhaps a small factory? Children were playing outside and bare-bottomed toddlers in the hallway. A fat woman with hair cascading down her back poked her head out of a half-open door. She had never heard of Detective Chief Inspector Maigret.

'Who do you want?'

'Mademoiselle Sabati.'

'Louise?'

'I think that's her name.'

'Go round the house and in through the back door, then up the stairs. There's only one door. It's there.'

He did as instructed, brushing against rubbish bins and stepping over refuse, the bugle call from the barracks ringing in his ears. The back door was open. A steep staircase with no handrail took him up to a floor on a different level from the others, and he knocked at a blue door.

At first there was no reply. He rapped harder and heard the shuffling of a woman in slippers, and had to knock a third time before she asked:

'What is it?'

'Mademoiselle Sabati?'

'What do you want?'

'To talk to you.'

He added on the off-chance:

'The doctor sent me.'

'Just a moment.'

She pattered away, probably to put on some suitable clothing. When she finally opened the door, she was wearing a cheap cotton dressing gown with a leaf pattern, beneath which she must only have had a nightdress. Her feet were bare inside her slippers, her black hair dishevelled.

'Were you asleep?'

'No.'

She looked him up and down warily. Behind her, at the end of a tiny hallway, was an untidy bedroom which she did not invite him to enter.

'What does *he* have to say to me?'

As she twisted her head slightly to one side, he noticed a bruise around her left eye. It wasn't entirely recent. The purple was beginning to turn yellow.

'Don't be frightened. I'm a friend. I simply wanted to talk to you for a few minutes.'

What must have decided her to let him in was the fact that two or three kids had come to gawp at them from the bottom of the stairs.

There were only two rooms, the bedroom, which he glimpsed with its unmade bed, and a kitchen. A novel lay open on the table next to a bowl containing the remains of a *café au lait*, and there was a portion of butter on a plate.

Louise Sabati was not beautiful. In a black dress and white apron, she must have had that weary look of most chambermaids in provincial hotels. Yet there was something appealing, almost pathetic, about her pale face and dark eyes with their intense expression.

She cleared a chair.

'Did Alain really send you?'

'No.'

'He doesn't know you're here?'

As she spoke, she darted a frightened glance towards the door. She remained standing, on the defensive.

'Don't be frightened.'

'Are you from the police?'

'Yes and no.'

'What's happened? Where's Alain?'

'At home, most likely.'

'Are you sure?'

'Why would he be anywhere else?'

She bit her lip and drew blood. She was very anxious, pathologically anxious. For a moment, he wondered whether she was a drug addict.

'Who told you about me?'

'How long have you been the doctor's mistress?'

'Someone told you?'

He put on his sincerest manner and it was no effort for him to be kind to her.

'Have you only just got up?' he asked, instead of replying.

'What business is it of yours?'

She still had a trace of an Italian accent. She couldn't be much more than twenty and her body, beneath the ill-fitting dressing gown, was curvaceous; only her breasts, which must have been provocative, were sagging a little.

'Would you mind sitting down?'

She was unable to keep still. She frantically grabbed a cigarette and lit it.

'Are you sure Alain isn't coming?'

'Are you afraid he will? Why?'

'He's jealous.'

'He has no reason to be jealous of me.'

'He's jealous of all men.'

She added in a strange voice:

'So he should be.'

'What do you mean?'

'That's his right.'

'Does he love you?'

'I think so. I don't know if I deserve it, but . . .'

'Won't you sit down?'

'Who are you?'

'Detective Chief Inspector Maigret, of the Paris Police Judiciaire.'

'I've heard of you. What are you doing here?'

Why not be open with her?

'I came here by coincidence, to visit a friend I hadn't seen for years.'

'Was he the one who told you about me?'

'No. I also met your friend Alain. As a matter of fact, I've been invited to his house this evening.'

She could tell he was speaking the truth, but she still wasn't reassured. All the same, she pulled a chair towards her, although she didn't sit down straight away.

'He may not be in trouble at the moment, but he's likely to be very soon.'

'Why?'

From the way she asked, he deduced that she already knew.

'Some people think he may be the wanted man.'

'Because of the murders? It's not true. It's not him. He had no reason to—'

He interrupted her, holding out the anonymous letter the magistrate had handed over to him. She read it, her expression tense, frowning.

'I wonder who wrote that.'

'A woman.'

'Yes. And most likely a woman who lives here.'

'Why?'

'Because no one else knows. Not even in the house. I'd have sworn that no one knew who he was. It's spiteful, a dirty trick. Alain never—'

'Sit down.'

She finally did, carefully smoothing the folds of her dressing gown over her bare legs.

'How long have you been his mistress?'

She answered without hesitation:

'Eight months and one week.'

He suppressed a smile at her precision.

'How did it start?'

'I was working as a waitress at the Café de la Poste. He would come in from time to time, in the afternoon. He always sat at the same table by the window and watched the people going by. Everyone knew him and said hello to him, but he didn't find it easy to strike up conversations. After a while, I noticed he was watching me.'

She suddenly looked at him defiantly.

'Do you really want to know how it started? Well, I'll tell you! And you'll see he's not the man you think he is. After a while, he'd sometimes drop in for a drink in the evening. One night, he stayed until closing time. I tended to laugh at him, because of his big eyes that followed me everywhere. That night, I was seeing someone, the wine merchant who you're bound to meet. We turned right into the little street and—'

'And what?'

'Well! We cuddled up on a bench on the Champ-de-Mars, if you get my meaning. It never lasted long. When it was over, I left on my own to cross the square and go home, and I heard footsteps behind me. It was the doctor. I was a bit scared. I turned around and asked him what he wanted. He went all shamefaced and didn't know what to say. Do you know what he mumbled in the end? "Why did you do that?"

'And me, I burst out laughing: "Does it bother you?"

'"It upsets me deeply."

'"Why?"

'That was how he finally admitted that he was in love with me but had never dared tell me, and that he was very unhappy. Are you smiling?'

'No.'

It was true. Maigret wasn't smiling. He could picture Alain Vernoux in that situation.

'We walked until one or two o'clock in the morning, along the towpath, and in the end I was the one who was crying.'

'Did he come back here with you?'

'Not that night. It took a whole week. During those days, he spent nearly all his time at the café, watching me. He was even jealous seeing me say thank you to a customer when I was given a tip. He still is. He doesn't want me to go out.'

'Does he hit you?'

She instinctively raised her hand to the bruise on her cheek and, as her dressing gown sleeve rode up, he saw more bruises, as if her arms had been squeezed hard between powerful fingers.

'It's his right,' she replied, not without pride.

'Does it happen often?'

'Almost every time.'

'Why?'

'If you don't understand, I can't explain it to you. He loves me. He has to live in town, with his wife and children. He doesn't love his wife and he doesn't love his children either.'

'Did he tell you that?'

'I know it.'

'Are you unfaithful to him?'

She clammed up and glared fiercely at him. Then:

'Has someone told you?'

And, in a quieter voice:

'It did happen, at first, when I hadn't understood. I thought it was like with the others. When you start at fourteen, like me, you don't take it seriously. When he found out, I thought he was going to kill me. I'm not kidding. I've never seen such a terrifying man. He lay there on the bed for an hour, staring at the ceiling, his fists clenched, without saying a word, and I could tell he was very, very hurt.'

'Did you do it again?'

'Two or three times. I was a bit stupid.'

'And since?'

'No!'

'Does he come and see you every night?'

'Nearly every night.'

'Were you expecting him yesterday?'

She hesitated, wondering what her answers might divulge, wanting to protect Alain at all costs.

'What difference can that make?'

'You have to go out to buy food, don't you?'

'I don't go into town. There's a little grocer's on the corner of the street.'

'The rest of the time, you stay shut up in here?'

'I'm not shut up. I opened the door to you, didn't I?'

'He's never talked about locking you in?'

'How did you guess?'

'Did he do it?'

'For a week.'

'Did the neighbours notice?'

'Yes.'

'Is that why he let you have the key back?'

'I don't know. I don't get what you're driving at.'

'Do you love him?'

'Do you think I'd live this life if I didn't love him?'

'Does he give you money?'

'When he can.'

'I thought he was rich.'

'That's what everyone thinks, but he's in exactly the same situation as a young man who has to ask his father for a little money every week. They all live in the same house.'

'Why?'

'How do I know?'

'He could work.'

'That's his affair, isn't it? His father leaves him without any money for weeks on end.'

Maigret looked at the table, on which there was only bread and butter.

'Is that the case at the moment?'

She shrugged.

'What does it matter? Me too, I used to imagine things about people thought to be rich. It's all appearances! A big house with nothing in it. They're always bickering over scrounging a bit of money off the old man, and the trades-men sometimes have to wait months to get paid.'

'I thought Alain's wife was wealthy.'

'If she'd been wealthy, she wouldn't have married him. She reckoned he was. When she found out he wasn't, she started to hate him.'

There was a fairly lengthy silence. Maigret filled his pipe, slowly, dreamily.

'What are you thinking?' she asked.

'I think you truly love him.'

'Well, that's something!'

Her sarcasm was bitter.

'What I want to know,' she added, 'is why everyone's sud-denly against him. I read the paper. It doesn't say so directly, but I get the feeling he's under suspicion. Earlier, through the window I overheard women talking in the yard, very loudly, on purpose, to make sure I heard every word they were saying.'

'What were they saying?'

'That if the police were looking for a madman, they didn't need to look very far.'

'I presume they've heard the scenes at your place?'

'So what?'

She suddenly became enraged and got up from her chair.

'You too, because he loves a girl like me and because he's jealous, you're going to think he's crazy?'

Maigret rose and tried to calm her by putting his hand on her shoulder, but she pushed him away angrily.

'Say so, if that's what you think.'

'It is *not* what I think.'

'Do you think he's crazy?'

'Certainly not because he loves you.'

'But he's crazy anyway?'

'Until there's proof to the contrary, I have no reason to think he is.'

'And what's that supposed to mean, exactly?'

'It means that you are a good girl and—'

'I'm not a good girl. I'm a slut, a tramp, and I don't deserve—'

'You are a good girl and I promise to do my utmost to find the real culprit.'

'Are you certain it's not him?'

He exhaled, and began to light his pipe to hide his unease.

'You see, you don't dare say it!'

'You're a good girl, Louise. I'll probably come and see you again . . .'

But she had lost her trust in him and, closing the door behind him, she muttered:

'You and your promises!'

From the stairs, at the foot of which kids were watching him, he thought he heard her say to herself:

'You're just a stinking cop!'

5. The Game of Bridge

When they left the house in Rue Clemenceau at 8.15, they were so surprised by the calm and silence that suddenly enveloped them that they almost recoiled.

By around 5 p.m., the sky had become apocalyptically dark and it had been necessary for all the town's streetlamps to be lit. There had been two brief, dramatic rolls of thunder, and finally the heavens had opened, sending down not rain but hail. All the people in the street vanished, as if blown away by the wind, and white hailstones bounced off the cobbles like ping-pong balls.

Maigret, who at that moment had been in the Café de la Poste, had jumped to his feet like everyone else, and they all stood at the window watching the street the way people watch a fireworks display.

Now it was over and it was bewildering to hear neither the rain nor the wind, to walk through the still air and look up to see stars between the rooftops.

Perhaps because of the silence disturbed only by the sound of their footsteps, they walked without speaking, making their way up towards Place Viète. On the corner of the square, they brushed past a man standing stock-still in the dark, a white armband on his overcoat, a cosh in his hand, who was observing them without breathing a word.

A few steps further on, Maigret opened his mouth to ask a question and his friend, who had guessed it, explained in a constrained voice:

'The chief inspector telephoned me just before I left my chambers. It had been brewing since yesterday. This morning, kids went around putting notices in letterboxes. There was a meeting at six o'clock and *they* have set up a vigilance committee.'

They clearly did not mean the kids, but the town's hostile elements.

Chabot added:

'We can't stop them.'

There were three more vigilantes with armbands right outside the Vernoux's house in Rue Rabelais. They kept their eyes on Chabot and Maigret as they approached. They weren't patrolling but stood there on sentry duty. It was almost as if they were waiting for them and might stop them from going into the house. Maigret thought he recognized in the shortest of the three the lean shape of the teacher, Chalus.

They were quite intimidating. Chabot hesitated to go up to the house, and was probably tempted to carry on walking. It didn't feel like a riot yet, nor even a disturbance, but this was the first time they had come across such a tangible sign of popular discontent.

Outwardly calm, very dignified, not without a degree of solemnity, the investigating magistrate eventually mounted the steps and raised the door knocker.

Behind him, there wasn't a murmur, not a wisecrack. Still without moving, the three men stared after him.

The noise of the knocker echoed inside the house like in a church. At once, as if he had been waiting behind the door for them, a manservant drew back the chains and bolts and welcomed them with a silent bow.

This was obviously not the way things usually were, because Julien Chabot paused in the doorway of the drawing room, regretting perhaps that he had come.

In a room the size of a ballroom, the huge crystal chandelier was lit, other lamps blazed on the tables, and arranged in the various corners and around the fireplace were enough armchairs to seat forty people.

However, there was only one man there, at the far end of the room, Hubert Vernoux, with his white, silky hair, ensconced in a vast Louis XIII armchair. He rose to greet them, his hand outstretched.

'I told you yesterday, on the train, that you would come and see me, Monsieur Maigret. In fact, I telephoned our friend Chabot today to make sure that he would be bringing you.'

He was dressed in black, wearing what looked like a dinner jacket, with a monocle dangling from a ribbon on his chest.

'My family will be here in a minute. I don't understand why they haven't all come downstairs.'

In the dim train compartment, Maigret hadn't been able to see him clearly. Here, the man seemed older. When he had walked across the room, his gait had had the mechanical stiffness of an arthritis sufferer whose movements seem to be controlled by springs. His face was puffy and an almost artificial pink.

Why was Maigret reminded of an ageing actor determined to carry on in his role, living in the fear that the audience will notice that he's already half-dead?

'I'll have to let them know that you're here.'

He rang the bell and spoke to the manservant.

'Go and see if Madame is ready. And tell Mademoiselle Lucile, the doctor and Madame . . .'

Something was amiss. He was annoyed with his family for not being there. To put him at his ease, Chabot said, looking at the three bridge tables that had been laid out:

'Is Henri de Vergennes coming?'

'He telephoned me to apologize. The storm damaged the driveway of the château and it is impossible for him to get his car out.'

'Aumale?'

'The notary went down with flu this morning. He went to bed at lunchtime.'

In other words, no one would be coming. And it was as if the family too were loath to join them downstairs. The manservant did not reappear. Hubert Vernoux gestured towards the bottles on the table.

'Pour yourself a drink, would you? Please excuse me for a moment.'

Intending to fetch them himself, he went up the grand staircase with stone steps and a wrought-iron rail.

'How many people usually attend these bridge evenings?' asked Maigret quietly.

'Not many. About half a dozen, in addition to the family.'

'Who are normally in the drawing room when you arrive?'

Chabot nodded regretfully. Someone entered, noiselessly. Doctor Alain Vernoux, who hadn't dressed up and was sporting the same crumpled suit he'd worn that morning.

'Are you on your own?'

'Your father has just gone upstairs.'

'I passed him on the stairs. What about the ladies?'

'I think he's gone to call them.'

'I don't believe anyone else is coming.'

Alain turned his head towards the windows masked by heavy curtains.

'Did you see?'

And, knowing they understood what he meant:

'They're watching the house. Some of them must be standing guard outside the side door too. It's a very good thing.'

'Why?'

'Because, if there's another murder, people won't be able to say that it's someone in the house.'

'Do you think there'll be another murder?'

'If it's a madman, there's no reason for the killings to stop.'

Madame Vernoux, the doctor's mother, finally made her entrance, followed by her husband, who was slightly red in the face, as if he'd had to argue to persuade her to come downstairs. She was in her sixties, with hair that was still chestnut and dark rings around her eyes.

'Detective Chief Inspector Maigret of the Police Judiciaire in Paris.'

She inclined her head slightly and went to sit in an armchair that must have been hers. As she passed the magistrate, she said a curt:

'Good evening, Julien.'

Hubert Vernoux announced:

'My sister-in-law will be down right away. We had a power cut earlier, which delayed dinner. I imagine the electricity was off in the whole town?'

He was talking for the sake of it. The words didn't need to make any sense. He had to compensate for the emptiness of the drawing room.

'A cigar, inspector?'

For the second time since he had been in Fontenay, Maigret accepted, because he didn't dare take his pipe out of his pocket.

'Is your wife not coming down?'

'She's probably been detained by the children.'

It was already obvious that Isabelle Vernoux, the mother, had agreed to put in an appearance after goodness knows what bargaining, but that she was determined not to take an active part in the gathering. She had picked up a piece of needlepoint and paid no attention to what was being said.

'Do you play bridge, inspector?'

'I'm sorry to disappoint you, but I never play. Let me hasten to add that I greatly enjoy watching a game.'

Hubert Vernoux looked at the magistrate.

'How are we going to play? Lucile will definitely play. You and me. Alain, I suppose—'

'No. Don't count on me.'

'There's still your wife. Do you want to go and see if she's ready?'

This was becoming painful. No one would sit down, apart from the mistress of the house. Maigret's cigar gave him an air of composure. Hubert Vernoux had lit one too and busied himself pouring brandies.

Could the three men on guard outside imagine the scene inside?

Lucile came down at last. She was a thinner, bonier replica of her sister. She also only glanced briefly at Maigret and walked straight over to the bridge tables.

'Shall we start?' she asked.

Then, gesturing vaguely in Maigret's direction:

'Does he play?'

'No.'

'So who's playing, then? Why was I asked to come down?'

'Alain has gone to fetch his wife.'

'She won't be joining us.'

'Why not?'

'Because she's got her neuralgia. The children were insufferable all evening. The governess handed in her notice and left. Jeanne's looking after the baby . . .'

Hubert Vernoux mopped his forehead.

'Alain will persuade her.'

And, turning towards Maigret:

'I don't know whether you have children. It's probably like this in all large families. Every child is out for themselves. Each has their own activities, their preferences . . .'

He was right: Alain walked in with his wife, a nondescript woman, on the plump side, with eyes red from crying.

'I'm sorry,' she said to her father-in-law. 'The children were playing up.'

'I hear the governess—'

'We'll talk about it tomorrow.'

'Detective Chief Inspector Maigret—'

'Pleased to meet you.'

She held out her hand, but it was limp, without warmth.

'Are we playing?'

'We're playing.'

'Who?'

'Are you absolutely sure, Inspector, that you don't wish to join in?'

'Certain.'

Julien Chabot, perfectly at home, was already seated and was shuffling the cards. He spread them on the green baize.

'Your turn to draw, Lucile.'

She turned over a king, her brother-in-law a jack. The magistrate and Alain's wife drew a three and a seven.

'We're partners.'

It had taken nearly half an hour, but at last they were settled. In her corner, Isabelle Vernoux senior continued to ignore them all. Maigret was sitting at a distance, behind Hubert Vernoux, whose hand he could see as well as that of his daughter-in-law.

'Pass.'

'One club.'

'Pass.'

'One heart.'

The doctor appeared not to know what to do with himself and was still standing. Everyone was under orders. Hubert Vernoux had gathered them together, almost by force, to keep up the semblance of normal life in the house, perhaps to impress Maigret.

'Well! Hubert?'

His sister-in-law, who was his partner, was taking him to task.

'I'm sorry! . . . Two clubs . . .'

'Are you sure you don't mean three? I bid a heart over your club, which means I have at least two and a half honours . . .'

From that moment, Maigret began to take a keen interest in the game. Not for the game itself, but for what it revealed to him about the players' characters.

His friend Chabot, for instance, was as regular as a metronome, his bids exactly what they should have been, without brashness and without bashfulness. He played his hand calmly, made no comments to his partner. And when the young woman didn't give him the correct response, his face showed just the faintest hint of annoyance.

'I'm sorry, I should have said three spades.'

'It doesn't matter. You couldn't know what cards I have in my hand.'

In the third round, he bid and made a small slam, and apologized:

'Too easy. I was dealt it.'

The young woman, however, was distracted. She tried to get a grip on herself and, when it was her turn to play, she looked about her as if seeking help. She turned towards Maigret, her fingers on a card, to ask his advice.

She didn't like bridge, was only there because she had to be, to make up a fourth.

Lucile, on the other hand, dominated the table with her personality. It was she who, after each hand, commentated the game, chiding the others.

'Since Jeanne bid two hearts, you should have made a finesse. She obviously had the queen of hearts.'

What's more, she was right. She was always right. Her dark, beady eyes seemed to see through the cards.

'What's wrong with you today, Hubert?'

'But—'

'You're playing like a beginner. You barely seem to hear the bids. We could have won the hand by three no-trumps and you ask for four clubs which you won't make.'

'I was waiting for you to say it—'

'I wasn't going to tell you about my diamonds. It was up to you to . . .'

Hubert Vernoux tried to redeem himself. He was like those roulette players who, once they are losing, cling to the hope that their luck will turn any minute and try all the numbers, watching furiously as the winning numbers are the ones they have just dropped.

Nearly always, he bid higher than his hand, counting on his partner's cards, and, when they weren't forthcoming, he chewed the end of his cigar nervously.

'I assure you, Lucile, that I was perfectly within my rights in bidding two spades at the opening.'

'Except you didn't have either the ace of spades or the ace of diamonds.'

'But I had . . .'

He listed his cards, the blood rose to his face, while she gazed at him with icy fury.

To get himself back on an even keel, he bid even more recklessly, to the point where it was no longer bridge, but poker.

Alain had gone over to keep his mother company for a moment. He came back and stood behind the players, looking at the cards without interest, his large eyes blurred behind his glasses.

'Do you understand anything, inspector?'

'I know the rules. I'm able to follow the game, but not to play.'

'Do you find it interesting?'

'Very.'

He scrutinized Maigret more closely, realizing that Maigret's interest lay in the behaviour of the players much more than in the cards. He watched his aunt and his father with an annoyed air.

Chabot and Alain's wife won the first rubber.

'Shall we swap?' suggested Lucile.

'Unless we stay as we are and take our revenge.'

'I'd rather change partners.'

That was a mistake on her part. She ended up playing with Chabot, who never slipped up and whom it was impossible for her to criticize. Jeanne played badly. And perhaps because she invariably bid too low, Hubert Vernoux won the two rounds one after the other.

'It's pure luck.'

That was not entirely true. Admittedly, he had been dealt a good hand, But, if he had bid recklessly, he wouldn't have won because there was no hope to be had from his partner's cards.

'Shall we continue?'

'We'll finish the round.'

This time, Vernoux was with the magistrate, the two women together. And it was the men who won, with the result that Hubert Vernoux had won two games out of three.

He looked relieved, as if this game had mattered considerably to him. He mopped his forehead, went and poured himself a drink and took a glass over to Maigret.

'You see that despite what my sister-in-law says, I'm not so reckless. What she doesn't understand is that if you manage to grasp how your opponent's mind works, you've half-won the game, irrespective of the cards. The same applies to selling a farm or a piece of land. Understand how the buyer thinks and—'

'Please, Hubert.'

'What?'

'You could perhaps refrain from talking business here?'

'I apologize. I forget that women want us to make money, but they prefer not to know how.'

That too was unwise. His wife rebuked him from her distant armchair.

'Have you been drinking?'

Maigret had seen him drink three or four brandies. He had been struck by the way Vernoux furtively filled his glass, in haste, in the hope that his wife and his sister-in-law wouldn't notice. He downed the drink in one, then, to conceal his unease, filled Maigret's glass.

'I've only had two glasses.'

'They've gone to your head.'

'I think,' Chabot began, standing up and pulling his watch from his pocket, 'that it's time for us to leave.'

'It's barely half past ten.'

'You're forgetting that I have a lot of work. My friend Maigret must be feeling tired too.'

Alain looked disappointed. Maigret would have sworn that throughout the entire evening, the doctor had been hovering around him in the hope of having a quiet word with him.

The others did not detain them. Hubert Vernoux did not dare insist. What would happen when the players had left and he'd be alone facing the three women? Because Alain didn't count. That was obvious. No one had taken any notice of him. He would probably go up to his room or to his laboratory. His wife was more part of the family than he was.

In short, it was a family of women, as Maigret suddenly discovered. Hubert Vernoux had been allowed to play bridge provided he behaved himself, and they had watched him like a child.

Was that why, outside his home, he clung so desperately to the persona he had created for himself, fastidious about the slightest details of his dress?

Who knows? Maybe, earlier, when he had gone upstairs to fetch them, he had implored them to humour him, to allow him to act the master of the house and not humiliate him with their comments.

He had his eye on the brandy decanter.

'One more drink, inspector, what the English call a nightcap?'

Maigret didn't feel like another drink, but said yes to give him the opportunity to have one too. As Vernoux raised the glass to his lips Maigret caught his wife glaring at him, saw his hand waver and then, regretfully, put the glass down again.

When Chabot and Maigret reached the front door, where the manservant was waiting for them with their coats, Alain said quietly:

'I think I might walk some of the way with you.'

He didn't appear worried about the reaction of the women, who seemed surprised. His wife made no objection. She probably didn't care whether he went out or not, given the little importance he had in her life. She had moved closer to her mother-in-law and was admiring her work and nodding.

'You don't mind, inspector?'

'Not at all.'

The night air was cool, not chilly like the previous nights, and you wanted to fill your lungs with it and greet the stars that were back in the sky after such a long absence.

The three men with armbands were still outside, but this time they stepped back to make way. Alain hadn't put on an overcoat. As he passed the coat stand in the hall, he had put on a soft felt hat battered by the recent rains.

Seen like that, his body thrust forwards, his hands in his pockets, he looked more like a final-year student than a husband and a father.

They couldn't talk in Rue Rabelais, because voices carried a long way and they were aware of the presence of the three lookouts behind them. Alain jumped as he brushed against the one standing on the corner of Place Viète, whom he hadn't seen.

'I imagine they've put them all over town?' he muttered.

'Definitely. They're going to take turns.'

Few windows were still lit. People went to bed early. From a distance, at the far end of Rue de la République, they could see the lights of the Café de la Poste, which was still open, and two or three isolated passers-by, who vanished one after the other.

By the time they reached the magistrate's house, they hadn't had the time to exchange more than a few words. Chabot mumbled reluctantly:

'Are you coming in?'

Maigret said no:

'There's no point waking your mother.'

'She's not asleep. She never goes to bed before I get home.'

'We'll see one another tomorrow morning.'

'Here?'

'I'll drop into the courts.'

'I have to make a few telephone calls before I go to bed. There might be news.'

'Good night, Chabot.'

'Good night, Maigret. Good night, Alain.'

They shook hands. The key turned in the lock and a moment later the door closed again.

'Shall I walk you back to your hotel?'

They were the only people left in the street. A vision of the doctor whipping a hand out of his pocket and hitting him over the head with a hard object, a length of lead piping or a monkey wrench, flashed through Maigret's mind.

He replied:

'With pleasure.'

They set off. Alain couldn't muster the courage to speak straight away. When he did, it was to ask:

'What do you think?'

'About what?'

'About my father.'

What could Maigret have answered? What was interesting was the fact that the question was asked, that the young doctor had come out of his house purely to ask it.

'I don't think he's had a happy life,' muttered Maigret, without much conviction.

'Are there people who have happy lives?'

'At least momentarily. Are you unhappy, Docter Vernoux?'

'I don't count.'

'Yet you try to carve out your share of pleasure.'

The big eyes stared at him.

'What do you mean?'

'Nothing. Or, if you prefer, I'm saying that no one's entirely unhappy. Everyone clutches on to something, and creates a sort of happiness.'

'Do you realize what that means?'

And, since Maigret did not reply:

'Do you know that it is because of this search for what I would call the compensations, this search for some happiness in spite of everything, that obsessions are born, and often instability? The men who right now are drinking and playing cards at the Café de la Poste are trying to convince themselves that they are enjoying themselves.'

'What about you?'

'I don't understand the question.'

'Don't you seek compensations?'

This time, Alain was worried, suspecting Maigret of knowing more, but he was afraid to question him.

'Would you dare go over to the barracks neighbourhood tonight?'

It was rather out of pity that Maigret asked that, to dispel his doubts.

'You know?'

'Yes.'

'Have you spoken to her?'

'At length.'

'What did she tell you?'

'Everything.'

'Am I wrong?'

'I'm not judging you. You're the one who started talking about the instinctive search for compensations. What are your father's compensations?'

They had lowered their voices, because they had reached the open door of the hotel where a single lamp shone in the foyer.

'Why don't you reply?'

'Because I don't know the answer.'

'Does he not have affairs?'

'Definitely not in Fontenay. He's too well known and wouldn't be able to keep it a secret.'

'What about you. Do people know?'

'No. My case isn't the same. When my father goes to Paris or Bordeaux, I presume he has a bit of fun.'

He muttered to himself:

'Poor Papa!'

Maigret looked at him in surprise.

'Do you love your father?'

Modestly, Alain replied:

'At any rate, I feel sorry for him.'

'Has it always been like this?'

'It's been worse. My mother and my aunt have calmed down a little.'

'What have they got against him?'

'That he's a commoner, the son of a livestock merchant who used to get drunk in the village inns. The Courçons have never forgiven him for the fact that they needed him, do you see? And, in old Courçon's day, the situation was even harsher because Courçon was even more scathing than his daughters and his son Robert. Until my father's death, all the Courçons on earth will resent him for the fact that they are completely dependent on him financially.'

'And how do they treat you?'

'Like a Vernoux. And my wife, whose father was Viscount de Cadeuil, sides with my mother and my aunt.'

'Did you intend to tell me all that this evening?'

'I don't know.'

'You were anxious to talk to me about your father?'

'I wanted to know what you thought of him.'

'Weren't you chiefly worried about whether I knew about the existence of Louise Sabati?'

'How did you find out?'

'Through an anonymous letter.'

'Does the magistrate know? The police?'

'They aren't concerned.'

'But will they be?'

'Not if the murderer is found quickly. I have the letter in my pocket. I haven't told Chabot about my conversation with Louise.'

'Why not?'

'Because I don't think it is relevant at this stage of the investigation.'

'It's nothing to do with her.'

'Tell me, Doctor Vernoux—'

'Yes?'

'How old are you?'

'Thirty-six.'

'How old were you when you graduated?'

'I left medical school at twenty-five and then I was a junior doctor for two years at Sainte-Anne.'

'And you've never tried to earn your own living?'

He suddenly looked crestfallen.

'You aren't answering?'

'I have nothing to reply. You wouldn't understand.'

'Cowardice?'

'I knew you'd call it that.'

'And yet you didn't come back to Fontenay-le-Comte to protect your father?'

'You see, it's both simpler and more complicated. I came back one day for a few weeks' holiday.'

'And you stayed?'

'Yes.'

'Out of spinelessness?'

'If you like. Although that's not entirely true.'

'You felt unable to do anything else?'

Alain dropped the subject.

'How is Louise?'

'As always, I imagine.'

'Isn't she worried?'

'Is it a while since you've seen her?'

'Two days. I was planning to go and see her last night. But then I didn't dare. Today neither. Tonight it's worse, with the men patrolling the streets. Do you understand why the public started spreading rumours about us after the first murder?'

'It's a phenomenon I have frequently observed.'

'Why go for us?'

'Whom do you think they suspect, your father or you?'

'They don't care, so long as it's one of the family. My mother or my aunt would do just as well.'

They had to stop talking, because footsteps were approaching. They belonged to two men with armbands and coshes, who stared at them as they walked past. One of them shone the beam of an electric torch on them, saying loudly to his companion as they walked off:

'It's Maigret.'

'The other is the younger Vernoux.'

'I recognized him.'

Maigret advised Alain:

'You'd do better to go home.'

'Yes.'

'And not argue with them.'

'Thank you.'

'For what?'

'Nothing.'

He did not proffer his hand. His hat askew, he walked off, leaning forwards, in the direction of the bridge, and the patrol halted to watch him go past in silence.

Maigret shrugged, went inside the hotel and waited to be handed his key. There were two more letters for him, probably anonymous, but the paper was different, and so was the handwriting.

6. *The Ten-thirty Mass*

When he realized it was Sunday, he lingered in bed. Already before that he had been playing a secret childhood game. He sometimes still played it lying in bed next to his wife, taking care not to give anything away. And she would be duped, saying, as she brought him his coffee:

'What were you dreaming?'

'Why?'

'You were smiling in your sleep.'

That morning in Fontenay, before opening his eyes he sensed a ray of sunshine through his eyelids, whose delicate, tingling skin felt translucent. And probably because of the pulsing blood, it seemed of a brighter red than that of the sun in the sky – glorious, like in a painting.

He could create an entire world with that sun, showers of sparks, volcanoes, cascades of molten gold. He simply had to bat his eyelids gently, like a kaleidoscope, using his eyelashes as a grille.

He could hear pigeons cooing on a cornice above his window, then bells ringing in two places at once, and he pictured the tall bell-towers against a clear blue sky.

He continued with the game while listening to the noises from the street and then, from the echo of the footsteps, from a certain quality of silence, it dawned on him that it was Sunday.

He dallied for ages before stretching out his hand and picking up his watch from the bedside table. It showed 9.30. In Paris, on Boulevard Richard-Lenoir, if spring had also come at last, Madame Maigret in her dressing gown and slippers would have opened the windows and tidied the bedroom while a stew simmered on the stove.

He promised himself he would call her. Since there was no telephone in the room, he would have to wait until he went downstairs and phone her from the booth.

He pressed the electric bell. The chambermaid looked cleaner, more cheerful, than the previous day.

'What would you like to eat?'

'Nothing. I'd like a large pot of coffee.'

She had the same curious way of eying him.

'Shall I run you a bath?'

'Only once I've drunk my coffee.'

He lit a pipe and went to open the window. The air was still chilly, and he had to put on his dressing gown, but he could feel little waves of warmth. The façades and the cobblestones had dried. The street was empty, with the occasional family in their Sunday best walking past, or a village woman clasping a bunch of violets.

The pace of hotel life must have slowed down, because he waited a long time for his coffee. He had left the two letters received the previous evening on the bedside table. One was signed. The handwriting was as neat as on an engraving, in black ink, like Indian ink.

Has anyone told you that the widow Gibon was the midwife who delivered Madame Vernoux of her son Alain?

You might find that useful to know.

Regards.

Anselme Remouchamps

The second letter, anonymous, was written on luxury paper, the top of which had been cut off, probably to remove the letterhead. It was written in pencil.

Why not question the servants? They know more than anyone else.

On reading those words, the previous night before going to bed, Maigret had a hunch that they had been written by the manservant at Rue Rabelais who had wordlessly let him in and then handed him his overcoat when he left. The man, with dark hair and thick flesh, was aged between forty and fifty. He looked like the son of a tenant farmer who had not wanted to work the land and who harboured both hatred for the rich and contempt for the farming people he had come from.

It would probably be easy to obtain a sample of his handwriting. Perhaps, even, the paper belonged to the Vernoux family?

All that needed to be verified. In Paris, the task would have been easy. Here, ultimately, it was none of his business.

When the chambermaid came back at last with the coffee, he asked her:

'Are you from Fontenay?'

'I was born in Rue des Loges.'

'Do you know a certain Remouchamps?'

'The shoemaker?'

'His first name is Anselme.'

'He's the shoemaker who lives two doors down from my mother. He's got a wart on his nose as big as a pigeon's egg.'

'What kind of man is he?'

'He's been a widower for I don't know how many years – as long as I've known him, at any rate. He makes strange chortling noises at little girls to frighten them.'

She looked at him in surprise.

'You're smoking your pipe before you drink your coffee?'

'You can run my bath.'

He used the bathroom at the end of the corridor and lay in the hot water for a long time, daydreaming. Several times he opened his mouth as if to talk to his wife, whom he could usually hear bustling about in the adjacent bedroom while he took his bath at home.

It was 10.15 when he went downstairs. The owner was at the desk, in chef's whites.

'The investigating magistrate telephoned twice.'

'At what time?'

'The first time was just after nine o'clock, the second a few minutes ago. The second time I told him you'd be down any minute.'

'Could I put a call through to Paris?'

'On a Sunday, it shouldn't take long.'

He gave the number and went over to the doorway for a breath of air. There was no one watching him today. A cock crowed somewhere nearby, and the waters of the River Vendée could be heard gushing past. When an elderly woman in a purple hat passed by close to him, he could have sworn her clothes reeked of incense.

It was definitely Sunday.

'Hello! Is that you?'

'Are you still in Fontenay? Are you phoning me from Chabot's? How is his mother?'

Instead of replying, he asked:

'What's the weather like in Paris?'

'Since yesterday lunchtime, it's been spring.'

'Yesterday lunchtime?'

'Yes. It began right after lunch.'

He had missed half a day of sunshine!

'What about where you are?'

'It's a fine day too.'

'You haven't caught a cold?'

'I'm very well.'

'Are you coming home tomorrow morning?'

'I think so.'

'You're not certain? I thought—'

'I may be detained for a few hours.'

'By what?'

'Work.'

'You told me . . .'

. . . That he would take the opportunity to have a rest, of course! Wasn't he resting?

That was about all. They exchanged the customary phrases.

Next he called Chabot at home. Rose replied that the magistrate had left for the law courts at eight o'clock. He telephoned him there.

'Any news?'

'Yes. We've found the weapon. That's why I called you. I was told you were asleep. Can you hurry over?'

'I'll be there in a few minutes.'

'The doors are locked. I'll keep a lookout through the window and come down and open the door.'

'Is something wrong?'

Chabot sounded overwhelmed.

'I'll talk to you about it.'

Maigret took his time all the same. He wanted to relish the Sunday and he soon found himself ambling down Rue de la République where the Café de la Poste had already put its chairs and pedestal tables out on the terrace.

Two houses further down, the door of the patisserie was open and Maigret dawdled even more to inhale the delicious smell.

The bells rang. People began to appear in the street, more or less opposite Julien Chabot's house. It was the crowd emerging from the 10.30 mass at Notre-Dame. He had the impression that people weren't behaving exactly as they normally did on a Sunday. Very few worshippers set off for home immediately.

Huddles formed in the square, talking not animatedly but in hushed tones, often falling silent as they glanced towards the doors from which the tide of parishioners was pouring. Even the women lingered, clutching their gilt-edged prayer books in their gloved hands, nearly all of them wearing pastel-coloured spring hats.

A long, gleaming car was parked in front of the church square and, standing by the door, there was a chauffeur in black livery whom Maigret recognized as the Vernoux's manservant.

Was the family, who lived no more than 400 metres away, in the habit of being driven to church by car? It was possible.

Maybe it was part of their tradition. It was possible too that they had taken the car today to avoid contact with inquisitive people in the streets.

They were coming out now, and Hubert Vernoux's white head stood out above the others. He walked slowly, his hat in his hand. When he was at the top of the steps, Maigret recognized at his side his wife, his sister-in-law and his daughter-in-law.

The crowd parted imperceptibly. They didn't form a guard of honour exactly, but there was an empty space around the family group and all eyes were on them.

The chauffeur opened the door. The women got in first. Then Hubert Vernoux sat in the front and the limousine glided off in the direction of Place Viète.

Perhaps at that moment, a word yelled by someone in the crowd, a shout, a gesture, would have been enough to spark off the people's anger. Elsewhere but at the church doors, that might well have happened. Expressions were grim, and although the clouds had gone from the sky, the air was heavy with anxiety.

A few people shyly greeted Maigret. Did they trust him still? They watched him walk up the street, his pipe in his mouth and his shoulders hunched.

He walked around Place Viète and turned into Rue Rabelais. Opposite the Vernoux's, on the other side of the street, two young men not even twenty years old were standing guard. They weren't wearing armbands, didn't have coshes. Those accoutrements seemed to be reserved for the night patrols. But they were still under orders and looked proud to be so.

One raised his cap as Maigret walked past, the other didn't.

Half a dozen or so journalists were gathered on the steps of the law courts, whose massive doors were closed, and Lomel had sat down, his cameras next to him.

'Do you think they're going to let you in?' he shouted at Maigret. 'You've heard the news?'

'What news?'

'Apparently they've found the weapon. They're having big talks in there.'

The door opened a fraction. Chabot signalled to Maigret to come inside quickly and, as soon as he was in, pushed back the door as if he feared the reporters would storm the building.

The corridors were drab and the stone walls exuded all the dampness of the past weeks.

'I would have liked to speak to you in private first, but it wasn't possible.'

There was light in the magistrate's chambers. The prosecutor was there, sitting on a chair which he tilted backwards, a cigarette in his mouth. Chief Inspector Féron was there too, as well as Inspector Chabiron, who couldn't help giving Maigret a look that was both triumphant and mocking.

On the desk, Maigret immediately noticed a piece of lead piping around twenty-five centimetres in length and four centimetres in diameter.

'Is that it?'

They all nodded.

'No fingerprints?'

'Only traces of blood and two or three hairs stuck to it.'

The lenght of dark-green pipe had been part of a kitchen, cellar or garage system. The sections were distinct, probably made by a professional several months earlier, because the metal had had time to tarnish.

Had the length of piping been cut when a sink or another appliance had been moved? It was highly likely.

Maigret opened his mouth to ask where the object had been found when Chabot spoke:

'Tell us, inspector.'

That was the signal Chabiron had been waiting for. Putting on a modest air he gave his account:

'We Poitiers police still use the good old methods. Not only did my partner and I question all the residents in the street, but I also searched high and low. A few metres from the spot where Gobillard was attacked, there's a big door that leads into a courtyard belonging to a horse trader, with stables all around it. This morning, my curiosity prompted me to go and have a look around. And I soon came across this object buried in the manure on the ground. In all probability, on hearing footsteps, the murderer threw it over the wall.'

'Who examined it for fingerprints?'

'I did. Inspector Féron helped me. We may not be experts, but we know enough to take fingerprints. It's certain that Gobillard's killer wore gloves. As for the hairs, we went to the morgue to check them against the dead man's hair.'

He concluded smugly:

'They match.'

Maigret refrained from giving an opinion. There was a silence, which the magistrate eventually broke.

'We were discussing what is the best thing to do now. This discovery seems to bear out Émile Chalus' statement, at least at first sight.'

Maigret still said nothing.

'Had the weapon not been discovered at the scene, it could have been argued that the doctor would have found it hard to get rid of before going to telephone from the Café de la Poste. As the inspector so reasonably pointed out.'

Chabiron preferred to speak his own mind:

'Let us assume that the killer really had got away once he'd committed the murder, before the arrival of Alain Vernoux, as Vernoux claims. It is his third murder. On the other two occasions, he kept his weapon with him. Not only did we find nothing in Rue Rabelais, nor in Rue des Loges, but it seems clear that he struck three times with the same length of lead piping.'

Maigret had fathomed that, but it was better to let Chabiron go on.

'The man had no reason, this time, to throw his weapon over the wall. He wasn't being followed. No one had seen him. But if we accept that it was the doctor who killed, it was vital for him to get rid of such a compromising object before—'

'Why alert the authorities?'

'Because that put him out of the frame. He thought that no one would suspect the person who raised the alarm.'

'That makes sense too.'

'That's not all. As you know.'

He had spoken those last words with a certain embarrassment, because Maigret, although not his direct superior, was still a big name whom you didn't challenge to his face.

'Go on, Féron.'

The police inspector, self-conscious, first stubbed out his cigarette in the ashtray. Chabot looked glum and avoided meeting his friend's eye. Only the prosecutor glanced at his wristwatch from time to time, like a man who had more enjoyable things to do.

After clearing his throat, the diminutive police inspector turned to Maigret.

'When I received the phone call yesterday, asking me if I knew a certain Sabati girl . . .'

Maigret understood and was suddenly afraid. He felt an unpleasant contraction in his chest and his pipe began to have a nasty taste.

' . . . I naturally wondered if there was a connection with the case. It came back to me in the middle of the afternoon. I was busy. I nearly sent one of my men, then I said to myself that I'd drop in to see her on the off-chance on my way to dinner.'

'Did you go?'

'I found out that you had seen her before I did.'

Féron bowed his head, like a man loath to make an accusation.

'Did she tell you?'

'Not right away. At first she refused to open the door to me and I had to take drastic steps.'

'Did you threaten her?'

'I told her it could cost her dearly to play that game. She let me in. I noticed her black eye and asked her who had given it to her. For over half an hour she sat there as tight as a clam, watching me with contempt. That's when I decided to take her down to the station, where it's easier to get people to talk.'

Maigret had a weight on his shoulders, not only because of what had happened to Louise Sabati, but because of the chief inspector's attitude. Despite his hesitations, his apparent humility, deep down Féron was very proud of what he had done.

It was clear he had blithely attacked this simple girl who had no means of defence. Even though he himself was probably from a lower-class background, he had lashed out at one of his own people.

Nearly everything he was saying now, in a voice that was growing increasingly confident, was painful to hear.

'Given that she hasn't worked for more than eight months now, she is officially without means, and that's the first thing I pointed out to her. And, since she regularly entertains a man, that classes her as a prostitute. She got it. She was frightened. She resisted for a long time. I don't know how you managed it, but eventually she told me everything she'd told you.'

'What was that?'

'Her relationship with Alain Vernoux, his behaviour, his fits of blind rage and beating her up.'

'Did she spend the night in the cells?'

'I let her go this morning. It did her good.'

'Did she sign her statement?'

'I wouldn't have let her leave if she hadn't.'

Chabot gave his friend a reproving look.

'I knew nothing of all this,' he muttered.

He must have told them that already. Maigret hadn't talked to him about his visit to the barracks neighbourhood, and now the magistrate must be thinking that this omission, which put him in a tricky situation, was a betrayal.

Maigret remained outwardly calm. His gaze lighted on the puny inspector who seemed to be expecting praise.

'I presume you have drawn conclusions from this business?'

'In any case it shows Doctor Vernoux in a new light. Early this morning, I questioned the neighbours, who confirmed that on almost every one of his visits, there'd been violent scenes in the room, and on several occasions they'd nearly called the police.'

'Why didn't they?'

'Most likely because they thought it was none of their business.'

No! If the neighbours didn't raise the alarm, it was because they were getting their own back on the Sabati girl, who had nothing to do all day long. And, probably, the harder Alain hit her, the happier they were.

They could have been the sisters of the feeble Inspector Féron.

'What became of her?'

'I ordered her to go home and remain at the disposal of the investigating magistrate.'

Now Chabot cleared his throat.

'It is undeniable that this morning's two revelations put Alain Vernoux in a difficult situation.'

'What did he do last night, after he left me?'

It was Féron who replied:

'He returned home. I'm in touch with the vigilance committee. Since I couldn't prevent this committee from being established, I prefer to be assured of its collaboration. Vernoux went straight back home.'

'Is he in the habit of attending the ten-thirty mass?'

This time Chabot replied:

'He doesn't go to mass at all. He's the only one in his family who doesn't.'

'Did he go out this morning?'

Féron gave a vague wave of his hand.

'I don't think so. At half past nine, nothing had been reported to me yet.'

The prosecutor finally spoke, sounding like a man who was beginning to weary of the whole business.

'All this is getting us nowhere. What we need to know is whether we have sufficient evidence against Alain Vernoux to arrest him.'

He stared hard at the magistrate.

'Over to you, Chabot. That's your responsibility.'

Chabot was looking at Maigret, whose expression was solemn and neutral.

Then, instead of a reply, the investigating magistrate made a speech.

'The situation is this. For one reason or another, public opinion pointed to Alain Vernoux from the first murder, that of his uncle Robert de Courçon. I still wonder what people based their accusations on. Alain Vernoux is not well liked. His family is more or less loathed. I have received some twenty anonymous letters naming the house in Rue Rabelais and accusing me of making allowances for the wealthy whose society I keep.

'The other two murders did not allay these suspicions, on the contrary. For a long time, some people have considered Alain Vernoux to be "different from everyone else".'

Féron broke in:

'The Sabati girl's statement—'

'—is damning for him, as is that of Chalus, now that the weapon has been found. Three murders in one week is a lot. It is natural for the townspeople to be worried and to seek to protect themselves. Until now, I've been reluctant to act, judging the evidence insufficient. It is indeed a huge responsibility, as the prosecutor pointed out. Once under arrest, a man of Vernoux's character, even if guilty, will remain silent.'

He caught a smile on Maigret's lips that was not without irony or bitterness, turned red and lost his train of thought.

'It is a matter of deciding whether it would be best to arrest him now or to wait until . . .'

Maigret couldn't help muttering under his breath:

'Well, no one had any qualms about arresting the Sabati girl and holding her overnight!'

Chabot heard him, opened his mouth to reply, most likely to retort that it wasn't the same thing, but thought better of it at the last minute.

'This morning, because of the Sunday sunshine, because of mass, we are witnessing a sort of truce. But, already at this hour, over an aperitif in the cafés, people are bound to be talking again. Those out for a stroll will deliberately walk past the Vernoux's residence. They know we played bridge there last night and that Inspector Maigret was with me. It's hard to get them to understand—'

'Are you going to arrest him?' asked the prosecutor, rising to his feet, judging that the dithering had gone on long enough.

'I'm afraid that there might be an incident towards evening that could have serious consequences. It would take very little, a kid throwing a stone at the windows, a drunkard shouting abuse outside the house. Given the current mood—'

'Are you going to arrest him?'

The prosecutor looked around for his hat, couldn't find it. The Féron said to him in a servile tone:

'You left it in your office. I'll go and fetch it for you.'

And Chabot, turning towards Maigret, grunted:

'What do you think?'

'Nothing.'

'In my shoes, what would—?'

'I'm not in your shoes.'

'Do you think the doctor is mad?'

'It depends what you call mad.'

'That he killed?'

Maigret did not reply but started looking for his hat too.

'Wait a minute. I need to talk to you. First of all, I have to put an end to this. Too bad if I'm wrong.'

He opened the right-hand drawer and took out a printed form, which he started to complete while Chabiron shot Maigret a glance that was even more disdainful.

Chabiron and the puny chief inspector had won. The form was a bench warrant. Chabot wavered for a second before signing and stamping it.

Then he wondered which of the two men to give it to. There had never been a case of an arrest like this in Fontenay.

'I suppose . . .'

Finally:

'Actually, both of you go. As discreetly as possible, to avoid any protests. You'd better take a car.'

'I have mine,' said Chabiron.

It was an unpleasant moment. Fleetingly, it seemed as if each of them was a little ashamed. Perhaps not so much because they doubted the doctor's guilt, of which they were almost certain, but because they knew, deep in their hearts, that they were acting chiefly out of fear of public opinion.

'Keep me posted,' said the prosecutor, who was the first to leave, adding: 'If I'm not at home, call me at my parents-in-law's'.

He was going to spend the rest of the Sunday with his family. Then Féron and Chabiron left, the carefully folded warrant in the short inspector's wallet.

Chabiron retraced his steps after glancing out of the corridor window to ask:

'What about the press?'

'Don't say anything to them now. Head for the centre of town first. Tell them that I'll have an announcement to make in half an hour and they'll stay put.'

'Shall we bring him here?'

'Take him straight to the prison. If the crowd tries to lynch him, it will be easier to protect him there.'

All that took time. They were finally alone. Chabot was not proud of himself.

'What do you think?' he finally asked. 'Do you think I'm making a mistake?'

'I am afraid,' admitted Maigret who was smoking his pipe gloomily.

'Of what?'

He did not reply.

'In all conscience, I couldn't do otherwise.'

'I know. That's not what I'm thinking about.'

'What are you thinking about?'

He did not want to admit that it was the attitude of the little inspector towards Louise Sabati that he found hard to stomach.

Chabot looked at his watch.

'In half an hour it will be over. We'll be able to go and question him.'

Maigret still said nothing, appearing to pursue who-knows-what mysterious thoughts.

'Why didn't you talk to me about it last night?'

'About the Sabati girl?'

'Yes.'

'To avoid what has happened.'

'It happened regardless.'

'Yes. I hadn't foreseen that Féron would take an interest in her.'

'Do you have the letter?'

'What letter?'

'The anonymous letter I received about her and which I gave you. Now I have to put it in the file.'

Maigret rummaged in his pockets and found it, crumpled, still damp from the previous day's rain, and dropped it on to the desk.

'Would you have a look and see if the journalists followed them?'

He went and peered out of the window. The reporters and photographers were still there, with an air of expectancy.

'Have you got the right time?'

'Five past twelve.'

They hadn't heard the bells chime midday. With all the doors closed, it was as if they were in a cellar where no ray of sunshine penetrated.

'I wonder how he'll react. I also wonder what his father—'

The telephone rang. Chabot was so startled that he sat there for a moment without picking it up, and mumbled eventually, gazing at Maigret:

'Hello . . .'

His forehead furrowed, his eyebrows knitted:

'Are you certain?'

Maigret heard shouting at the other end of the line, but was unable to make out what was being said. It was Chabiron who was speaking.

'Have you searched the house? Where are you now? Good. Stay there. I . . .'

Frazzled, Chabot wiped his hand over his head.

'I'll call you back in a moment.'

When he hung up, Maigret merely said one word.

'Gone?'

'Were you expecting it?'

And, since he did not reply:

'He went home last night after leaving you, that we know. He spent the night in his room. Early this morning, he had a cup of coffee brought up.'

'And the papers.'

'There aren't any papers on Sunday.'

'Who did he talk to?'

'I don't know yet. Féron and Chabiron are still at the house questioning the servants. A little after ten o'clock, the entire family except Alain went to mass in the car, driven by the manservant.'

'I saw them.'

'On their return, no one was worried about the doctor. It is a household where, apart from Saturday evenings, everyone leads their own separate life. When my two men arrived, a maid went upstairs to inform Alain. He wasn't in his apartment. They called him all over the house. Do you think he ran away?'

'What does the man on guard duty outside say?'

'Féron questioned him. The doctor reportedly went out shortly after the rest of the family and walked into town.'

'Didn't anyone follow him? I thought—'

'I had given instructions for him to be followed. I don't know, maybe the police thought it was unnecessary on a Sunday morning. If we don't lay our hands on him, people will say I deliberately gave him time to get away.'

'They definitely will.'

'There are no trains before five o'clock this afternoon. Alain doesn't have a car.'

'So he can't be far away.'

'Do you think?'

'I wouldn't be surprised if he were found at his mistress's. Normally he only slips out to see her in the evening, under cover of the dark. But he hasn't been for three days.'

Maigret did not add that Alain knew he paid her a visit.

'What's wrong?' asked the investigating magistrate.

'Nothing. I'm afraid, that's all. You'd do better to send them over there.'

Chabot telephoned. After which the two of them sat facing one another, in silence, in the chambers where spring had not yet arrived, the glow from the green lampshade making them look sickly.

7. Louise's Treasure

While they were waiting, Maigret suddenly had the disconcerting impression that he was looking at his friend under a magnifying glass. Chabot seemed even older, more subdued than when he had arrived two days earlier. There was just enough life in him, enough energy, enough personality to live the life he led, but when he was unexpectedly required to put in an extra effort, as was the case now, he went to pieces, ashamed of his inertia.

But Maigret was convinced it was not a question of age. He must always have been like that. It was Maigret who had been wrong, in the past, in the days when they were students and he had envied his friend. Then, he had seen Chabot as the embodiment of the happy adolescent. In Fontenay, a mother who fussed over him welcomed him in a comfortable house where things seemed solid and permanent. He knew he would inherit two or three farms in addition to this house, and he was given enough money every month to lend some to his friends.

Thirty years had passed and Chabot had become what he was destined to become. And today, he was the one turning to Maigret for help.

The minutes went by. The magistrate pretended to flick through a file, but his eyes were not following the typewritten lines. The telephone remained obstinately silent.

He drew his watch out of his pocket.

'It doesn't take five minutes to drive there. Or to drive back. They should . . .'

It was 12.15. The two police officers needed a few minutes to go and look around the house.

'If he doesn't confess, and if in two or three days I haven't found incontrovertible evidence, I'll have no option but to put in for early retirement.'

He had acted out of fear of the majority of the townsfolk. But now he was frightened of the reactions of the Vernoux family and their ilk.

'Twenty past twelve. What on earth are they doing?'

At 12.25, he got up, too anxious to sit still.

'Don't you have a car?' Maigret asked.

He looked embarrassed.

'I used to have one that I drove on Sundays to take my mother for a spin in the country.'

It was funny hearing someone who lived in a town where cows grazed 500 metres from the main square talking about the country.

'Now that my mother only goes out to attend Sunday mass, what would I do with a car?'

Perhaps he had become tight-fisted? It was likely. Not necessarily through any fault of his. When a person has a small fortune, as he did, they are inevitably afraid of losing it.

Since his arrival in Fontenay, Maigret had had the impression that he understood things he had never thought about before, and he built up a picture of a small town that was different from how he had previously imagined it.

'There's bound to be some news.'

The two police officers had been gone more than twenty minutes. It wouldn't take long to search Louise Sabati's two-roomed lodging. Alain Vernoux was not the sort of man to escape through the window and it was hard to envisage a manhunt in the streets of the barracks neighbourhood.

There was a moment of hope when they heard a car engine approaching and the magistrate remained stock-still in expectation, but the car continued up the hill without stopping.

'I don't understand.'

He pulled on his long fingers covered in blond hairs, darting brief glances at Maigret as if begging for reassurance, but Maigret remained resolutely expressionless.

When, shortly after 12.30, the telephone rang at last, Chabot literally threw himself at the instrument.

'Hello!' he bawled.

But he was immediately disappointed. It was a woman calling, a woman who sounded unused to making phone calls. She was shouting so loudly that Maigret could hear her from the other side of the room.

'Is that the magistrate?' she asked.

'Investigating magistrate Chabot, yes. How can I help?'

She repeated just as loudly:

'Is that the magistrate?'

'Speaking. What do you want?'

'Are you the magistrate?'

And he, furious:

'Yes. I am the magistrate. Can't you hear me?'

'No.'

'What do you want?'

If she had asked him one more time if he was the magistrate, he would probably have flung the telephone on to the floor.

'The inspector wants you to come.'

'What?'

But now, talking to someone else in the room from which she was telephoning, she said in a different tone:

'I told him. What?'

A voice commanded:

'Hang up.'

'Hang what up?'

There was a racket coming from the law courts. Chabot and Maigret listened out.

'Someone's banging on the door.'

'Come on.'

They raced down the corridors. The din was even louder. Chabot hurriedly drew back the bolts and turned the key in the lock.

'Did someone call you?'

It was Lomel, surrounded by three or four fellow journalists. Others could be seen running down the street towards the open countryside.

'Chabiron has just driven past in his car. There was an unconscious woman next to him. He must be taking her to the hospital.'

A car was parked at the foot of the steps.

'Whose is it?'

'Mine, or rather my newspaper's,' said a reporter from Bordeaux.

'Drive us.'

'To the hospital?'

'No. Drive to Rue de la République first of all then turn right, towards the barracks.'

They piled into the car. Outside the Vernoux's house, a knot of around twenty people had formed and they watched the car go by in silence.

'What's going on, sir?' asked Lomel.

'I don't know. We were about to make an arrest.'

'The doctor?'

He didn't have the heart to deny it, or to play games. A few people were sitting on the terrace of the Café de la Poste. A woman in her Sunday best was coming out of the patisserie, dangling a white cardboard box from a red ribbon.

'Down here?'

'Yes. Now, left . . . Wait . . . Turn after this building . . .'

There was no mistaking it. In front of the house where Louise had lodgings a crowd had gathered, mainly women and children, who ran over to the doors when the car pulled up. The fat woman who had given Maigret directions the previous day was standing at their head, her hands on her hips.

'It's me who went and phoned you from the grocer's. The inspector's up there.'

There was a lot of confusion. The little troop made their way to the rear of the house with Maigret, who knew his way around, at their head.

Around the back of the building they found even more curious onlookers who were blocking the door. There were even people on the stairs, at the top of which the puny police inspector was forced to stand guard in front of the broken-down door.

'Make way please . . . Stand aside . . .'

Féron's face was haggard, his hair tumbling on to his fore-head. He had lost his hat. He looked relieved to see reinforcements arriving.

'Have you told the police station to send me more men?'

'I didn't know that—' began Chabot.

'I asked that woman to tell you—'

The journalists were trying to take photos. A baby was crying. Chabot, whom Maigret had allowed to go ahead of him, reached the top of the stairs, asking:

'What's going on?'

'He's dead.'

He pushed the door, which had splintered into pieces.

'In the bedroom.'

The room was a mess. The open window let in the sun and the flies.

On the unmade bed, Doctor Alain Vernoux lay fully dressed, his spectacles on the pillow next to his face, from which the blood had already drained.

'Tell us, Féron.'

'There's nothing to tell. We got here, the inspector and myself, and people showed us to this staircase. We knocked. Since no one replied, I gave the usual orders. Chabiron put his shoulder to the door and gave two or three hard shoves. We found him like this, lying where he is. I felt his pulse. It was not beating. I held a mirror in front of his mouth.'

'What about the girl?'

'She was on the floor, as if she'd slid off the bed, and she had vomited.'

They were all stepping in the pool of vomit.

'She wasn't moving, but she's not dead. There's no telephone in the house. I couldn't comb the neighbourhood looking for one. Chabiron put her over his shoulder and took her to the hospital. There was nothing else to be done.'

'Are you certain she was breathing?'

'Yes, with a strange rattle in her throat.'

The photographers were still at work. Lomel was scribbling in a little red notebook.

'The entire household was on my back. At one point, some kids managed to slip into the room. I couldn't leave. I wanted to let you know. I sent the woman who seems to act as the concierge and asked her to tell you . . .'

Indicating the mess around him, he added:

'I haven't even been able to look around the place.'

One of the journalists held out an empty vial of Veronal.

'In any case, there's this.'

That was the explanation. In Alain Vernoux's case, it was undoubtedly suicide.

Had he persuaded Louise to kill herself with him? Had he administered the drug to her without saying anything?

In the kitchen, there were the remains of a bowl of *café au lait* and a piece of cheese next to a slice of bread, and in the bread the girl's teeth marks.

She got up late and Alain Vernoux had probably found her having her breakfast.

'Was she dressed?'

'In her nightdress. Chabiron wrapped her in a blanket and carried her off as she was.'

'Did the neighbours hear them arguing?'

'I haven't had a chance to question them. The kids are all at the front of the crowd and the mothers aren't making any effort to shoo them away. Listen to them.'

One of the journalists leaned his back against the door, which would no longer close, to prevent people from pushing their way in.

Julien Chabot paced up and down as if in a nightmare, like a man who had lost control of the situation.

Two or three times, he moved closer to the body before plucking up the courage to touch the dangling wrist.

He repeated several times, forgetting that he had already said it, or as if trying to convince himself:

'It's obviously suicide.'

Then he asked:

'Shouldn't Chabiron be back by now?'

'I imagine he'll stay there to question the girl if she regains consciousness. We need to inform the police station. Chabiron promised to send me a doctor . . .'

Just then someone knocked at the door, and a young doctor walked straight over to the bed.

'Dead?'

Chabot nodded.

'How's the girl who was brought to you?'

'They're looking after her. There's a good chance she'll pull through.'

He looked at the vial, shrugged and muttered:

'Same thing again.'

'How come he's dead whereas she . . .?'

He pointed to the vomit on the floor.

One of the reporters, who had slipped away unnoticed, came back into the room.

'There was no argument,' he said. 'I questioned the neighbours. It's all the more certain because this morning most of the windows in the building were open.'

Meanwhile, Lomel was rummaging shamelessly through the drawers, which contained very little apart from some underwear, cheap clothes and knick-knacks of no value. Then he bent down to look under the bed, and Maigret saw him lie down on the floor, stretch out his arm and pull out a cardboard shoe-box tied up with a blue ribbon. Lomel withdrew to one side with his find and there was enough confusion in the room for him to be left in peace.

Only Maigret went over to him.

'What is it?'

'Letters.'

The box was almost full, not only of letters but also brief notes hastily scribbled on scraps of paper. Louise Sabati had kept everything, perhaps unbeknown to her lover, almost certainly in fact, otherwise she would not have hidden the box under the bed.

'Let me see.'

Lomel seemed upset on reading them. He said in a tremulous voice:

'They're love letters.'

The magistrate had finally become aware of what was going on.

'Letters?'

'Love letters.'

'From whom?'

'From Alain. Signed with his first name, sometimes only his initials.'

Maigret, who had read two or three of them, wanted to stop them being passed around. They were probably the most moving love letters he had ever read. The doctor had written them with the passion and sometimes the naivety of a twenty-year-old.

He called Louise: 'My little darling'.

Sometimes: 'My poor little darling'.

And he told her, like all lovers, how long the days and nights were without her, how empty life was, how empty the house, where he banged into the walls like a hornet; he told her he wished he had met her sooner, before any man had touched her, and about the rages he felt, alone in his bed at night, when he thought about the caresses she had endured.

At times, he spoke to her as if she were an irresponsible child, and at others his words were howls of hatred and despair.

'Gentlemen . . .' began Maigret, a lump in his throat.

No one took any notice of him. It was none of his business. Chabot, blushing, went on skimming through the letters, the lenses of his spectacles misty.

I left you half an hour ago and I'm back in my prison. I need to be close to you again . . .

He had known her for barely eight months. There were almost 200 letters and, some days, he had written three, one after the other. Some had no stamp. He must have brought them with him.

If I were man enough . . .

Maigret was relieved to hear the police arrive. They shepherded the crowd and the swarm of kids out of the way.

'You'd do better to remove them,' he whispered to his friend.

The letters had to be collected up from everyone in the room. The people who handed them over looked sheepish. Now they averted their gaze from the bed, and when they glanced at the body lying there, it was furtively, almost apologetically.

Like that, without his glasses, his face relaxed and peaceful, Alain Vernoux appeared ten years younger than he had done when alive.

'My mother must be getting worried,' said Chabot, checking his watch.

He was forgetting the house in Rue Rabelais where there was an entire family, a father, a mother, a wife, children, whom they were going to have to go and inform.

Maigret reminded him. The magistrate murmured:

'I'd much rather not go there myself.'

Maigret didn't dare offer. And perhaps his friend didn't dare ask.

'I'll send Féron.'

'Where?' asked the latter.

'Rue Rabelais, to inform them. Talk to his father first.'

'What shall I tell him?'

'The truth.'

The puny chief inspector muttered under his breath:

'Nice job!'

There was nothing more for them to do there. Nothing more to discover in the rooms of a poor girl whose box of letters was her only treasure. She probably hadn't understood all of them. It made no difference.

'Are you coming, Maigret?'

And, to the doctor:

'Will you arrange for the body to be removed?'

'To the morgue?'

'There'll have to be an autopsy. I don't see how . . .'

He turned to the two police officers.

'Don't let anyone in.'

He went down the stairs, the cardboard box under his arm, and had to push through the crowd gathered outside. He had not thought of the matter of a car. They were on the other side of town. Of his own accord, the journalist from Bordeaux hurried over.

'Where would you like me to drop you off?'

'At my house.'

'Rue Clemenceau?'

They drove most of the way in silence. It was only when they were within 100 metres of the house that Chabot murmured:

'I suppose that's the end of the case.'

He could not have been so certain because he studied Maigret covertly. And Maigret did not acquiesce. He said neither yes nor no.

'I don't see any reason, if he wasn't guilty, why . . .'

He clammed up, because on hearing the car, his mother, who must have been fretting, was already opening the door.

'I was wondering what's going on. I saw people running as if something had happened.'

Chabot thanked the reporter and felt obliged to offer:

'A quick drink?'

'No thank you. I have to call my paper urgently.'

'The roast will be overdone. I was expecting you at half past twelve. You look tired, Julien. Don't you think he looks under the weather, Jules?'

'You'll have to leave us for a moment, Mother.'

'Don't you want to eat?'

'Not straight away.'

She gripped Maigret.

'Nothing bad?'

'Nothing you need to worry about.'

He preferred to tell her the truth, or at least some of the truth.

'Alain Vernoux has committed suicide.'

She merely said:

'Oh!'

Then, shaking her head, she headed towards the kitchen.

'Let's go into my study. Unless you're hungry?'

'No.'

'Pour yourself a drink.'

He would have liked a beer, but he knew there wasn't any in the house. He opened the drinks cabinet and chose a bottle of Pernod at random.

'Rose will bring you some water and ice.'

Chabot had sunk into his armchair, where his father's head before his had made a dark stain on the leather. The shoe-box was on the desk, with the blue ribbon that had been retied.

The magistrate desperately needed reassurance. His nerves were frayed.

'Why don't you have a nightcap?'

From the look Chabot shot in the direction of the door, Maigret gathered that it was at his mother's insistence that he no longer drank.

'I'd rather not.'

'As you wish.'

Despite the mild temperature that day, there was still a fire burning in the hearth and Maigret, who was too warm, had to move away.

'What do you think?'

'About what?'

'About what he did. Why, if he wasn't guilty—'

'You read some of his letters, didn't you?'

Chabot bowed his head.

'Chief Inspector Féron burst into Louise's rooms yesterday, questioned her, took her to the police station and kept her in the cells all night.'

'He wasn't acting under my instructions.'

'I know. He did it anyway. This morning, Alain rushed over to see her and found out everything.'

'I don't see what difference that made.'

He had a very good idea, but didn't want to admit it.

'Do you think that's why . . . ?'

'I think it's enough. Tomorrow, the whole town would have known. Féron would probably have continued to harass the girl, and she'd have ended up being sentenced for prostitution.'

'He was rash. That's not a reason to kill oneself.'

'That depends on the person.'

'You're convinced he's not guilty.'

'What about you?'

'I think everyone will believe he's guilty and will be satisfied.'

Maigret looked at him in surprise.

'You mean you're going to close the case?'

'I don't know. I don't know any more.'

'Do you remember what Alain said to us?'

'About what?'

'That a madman has his own logic. A madman who has lived his entire life without anyone noticing his madness doesn't suddenly start killing for no reason. There has to be some provocation at least. There has to be a cause, which might not seem sufficient to a rational person, but which does to him.

'The first victim was Robert de Courçon and, in my view, that's the one that counts, because it's the only one that can provide us with a clue.

'Public speculation isn't born out of nothing either.'

'Do you trust the opinion of the masses?'

'They're sometimes misguided. But, as I've noticed over the years, there is nearly always a sound basis. I'd say that the crowd has an instinct—'

'So it is indeed Alain who—'

'That's not what I'm saying. When Robert de Courçon was killed, the townspeople made a connection between the two houses in Rue Rabelais and at that point no one was talking about madness. Courçon's murder wasn't necessarily the act of a madman or a maniac. There could have been specific reasons why someone decided to kill him, or did so in a moment of anger.'

'Go on.'

Chabot had no fight left. Maigret could have said anything to him and he would have agreed. He had the impression that it was his career, his life, that was being destroyed.

'I know no more than you do. There have been two more murders, one after the other, both inexplicable, both committed in the same way, as if the murderer wanted to underline that it was one and the same culprit.'

'I thought that criminals generally kept to one method, always the same.'

'I'm asking myself why he was in such a hurry.'

'Such a hurry to what?'

'To kill again. Then again. As if to firmly establish in the public mind that a maniac was at large.'

This time, Chabot looked up sharply.

'You mean he's not mad?'

'Not exactly.'

'So?'

'It's a question I regret not having discussed in more depth with Alain Vernoux. The little he said to us has stayed in my mind. Even a madman would not necessarily act like a madman.'

'That's obvious. Otherwise there wouldn't be any more lunatics on the loose.'

'Nor is it necessarily because he is mad that he kills.'

'You've lost me there. Your conclusion?'

'I don't have a conclusion.'

They jumped when the telephone rang. Chabot picked up the receiver, and his attitude and tone changed.

'Yes, madame. He is here. I'll put him on.'

And to Maigret:

'Your wife.'

On the other end of the line, Madame Maigret said:

'Is that you? I'm not disturbing your lunch? Are you still eating?'

'No.'

There was no point telling her he hadn't eaten yet.

'Your chief called me half an hour ago and asked if you would definitely be back tomorrow morning. I didn't know what to tell him because when you telephoned me, you didn't sound certain. He said that if I had the opportunity to phone you again, I should tell you that the daughter of some politician has been missing for two days. It's not in the papers yet. Apparently it's very important; there's likely to be an outcry. Do you know who it is?'

'No.'

'He mentioned a name but I've forgotten it.'

'In other words, he wants me back without fail?'

'He didn't say that. But I did gather that he wants you to handle the case in person.'

'Is it raining?'

'The weather's beautiful. Have you made up your mind?'

'I'll do my utmost to be in Paris tomorrow morning. There must be a night train. I haven't looked at the timetable yet.'

Chabot nodded to confirm that there was a night train.

'Is everything all right in Fontenay?'

'Everything is fine.'

'Give my regards to Julien Chabot.'

'I will.'

When he hung up, he couldn't have said whether his friend was sorry or delighted that he was leaving.

'Do you have to go back?'

'I have to do the right thing.'

'Perhaps it's time to sit down and have lunch?'

Reluctantly Maigret tore himself away from the white shoe-box that had a similar effect on him as a coffin.

'Let us not talk about it in front of my mother.'

They hadn't got to dessert yet when the front doorbell rang. Rose went to open the door, and came back to announce:

'It's the chief of police who's asking—'

'Show him into my study.'

'That's what I did. He's waiting. He says it's not urgent.'

Madame Chabot tried hard to make small talk as if nothing were amiss. She dredged up names from her memory, people who were dead, or who had moved away from the town years ago, reeling off their stories.

They finally left the table.

'Shall I have your coffees served in your study?'

Rose brought all three of them coffee and placed glasses and the bottle of brandy on the tray with an almost reverent gesture. They had to wait until the door closed behind her.

'Well?'

'I went there.'

'Cigar?'

'No thank you. I haven't had lunch yet.'

'Would you like me to ring for some food?'

'I telephoned my wife and told her I'd be home shortly.'

'How did it go?'

'The manservant opened the door and I asked if I could speak to Hubert Vernoux. He left me in the hall while he went to inform him. It took a long time. A boy of seven or eight came and stared at me from the top of the stairs and I heard his mother's voice calling him. Someone else was watching me through a half-open door, an old woman, but I don't know if it was Madame Vernoux or her sister.'

'What did Vernoux say?'

'He appeared at the end of the corridor and, when he was three or four metres from me, he asked, without stopping: "Have you found him?"

'I said that I had some bad news for him. He didn't invite me into the drawing room, but left me standing there on the mat, while he looked down on me, but I could see his lips and hands were trembling.

'"Your son is dead," I finally said.

'And he replied: "Did you kill him?"

'"He committed suicide, this morning, in his mistress's bedroom."'

'Did he seem surprised?' queried the investigating magistrate.

'I had the impression that it gave him a shock. He opened his mouth as if to ask a question, but merely muttered: "So, he had a mistress!"

'He didn't even ask who she was, or what had become of her. He headed towards the door to open it and his last words, as he dismissed me, were: "Maybe those people will leave us in peace now."

'He jerked his chin at the curious onlookers gathered on the pavement, the groups stationed on the opposite side of the street, the journalists who had taken advantage of his appearance on the doorstep to photograph him.'

'He didn't try to avoid them?'

'On the contrary. When he saw them, he lingered, facing them, looking them in the eyes, and then, slowly, he closed the door and I heard him drawing the bolts.'

'What about the girl?'

'I dropped in to the hospital. Chabiron is at her bedside. We don't know yet if she'll pull through, because she has some heart defect.'

Without touching his coffee, he knocked back the glass of brandy and stood up.

'Can I go and have lunch?'

Chabot nodded and rose to see him out.

'What do I do next?'

'I don't know yet. Come to my chambers. The prosecutor will be meeting me there at three o'clock.'

'I left two men outside the house in Rue Rabelais, just in case. Crowds of people are filing past, stopping to talk in undertones.'

'Are they calm?'

'Now that Alain Vernoux has killed himself, I don't think there's any more danger. You know how it is.'

Chabot looked at Maigret as if to say: 'You see!'

He would have given anything for his friend to reply: 'Of course. It's all over.'

Except that Maigret said nothing.

8. *The Invalid of Gros-Noyer*

Maigret had walked down the road from the Chabots' house, turning right shortly before the bridge, and for ten minutes he followed a long road that was neither town nor country.

At first, the white, red and grey houses, including the large residence and cellars of a wine merchant, were close together, but this street was very different in nature from Rue de la République, for instance, and some of the buildings, white-washed and single-storeyed, were almost cottages.

Then there were gaps, little alleys giving a glimpse of vegetable gardens sloping gently down to the river, sometimes a white goat tethered to a stake.

He met almost no one in the street, but through the open doors he caught sight of families who seemed motionless, listening to the radio or eating tart. In one house a man in shirt-sleeves sat reading the newspaper and, in another, a little old lady was snoozing beside a big grandfather clock with a brass pendulum.

The gardens gradually took over more and more , the gaps between the walls were wider, the Vendée flowed closer to the road, sweeping downriver the branches ripped off by the recent gales.

Maigret had refused to allow himself to be driven by car and now he was beginning to regret it because he hadn't realized it was such a long way, and the sun was already burning the back of his neck. It took him almost an hour to reach the Gros-Noyer crossroads, after which there seemed to be nothing but meadows.

Three youths dressed in navy blue, their hair brilliantined, were lolling against the door of an inn. They could not have known who he was, and watched him with the hostile disdain of villagers for the town-dweller lost among them.

'Madame Page's house?' he asked them.

'You mean Léontine?'

'I don't know her first name.'

That was enough to make them laugh. They found it funny that someone didn't know Léontine's first name.

'If it's her, go and knock on that door over there.'

The house they pointed to was only one-storeyed, and was so low that Maigret could reach up and touch the roof. The green door had two sections, like a stable door, the top half open and the bottom half closed.

At first he couldn't see anyone in the kitchen, which was very clean, with a white ceramic stove, a round table covered with a gingham oilcloth and lilacs in a colourful vase probably won at the fair; the mantelpiece was crammed with knick-knacks and photographs.

He rang a little bell hanging on a string.

'What is it?'

Maigret saw her come out of the bedroom whose door opened to the left: these were the only two rooms. The woman could have been any age between fifty and sixty-five. Blunt and hard, like the hotel chambermaid, she studied him with the suspicion of a countrywoman, without moving towards the door.

'What do you want?'

Followed immediately by:

'Aren't you the one whose picture's in the newspaper?'

Maigret heard a noise coming from the bedroom. A man's voice asked:

'Who is it, Léontine?'

'The inspector from Paris.'

'Detective Chief Inspector Maigret?'

'I think that's what he's called.'

'Let him in.'

Without moving, she repeated:

'Come in.'

Maigret drew back the bolt to open the bottom part of the door himself. Léontine did not invite him to sit down, remaining silent.

'You were Robert de Courçon's cleaner, weren't you?'

'For fifteen years. The police and the journalists have already asked me all the questions. I don't know anything.'

From where he stood, Maigret could now see a white room, its walls hung with colour prints and the foot of a walnut bed covered in a red eiderdown, and the smell of pipe smoke reached his nostrils. There were still sounds coming from within.

'I want to see what he's like,' mumbled the man.

And she, to Maigret, ungraciously:

'Do you hear what my husband says? Come in, he can't get up.'

The man sitting up in bed had a face devoured by his beard; newspapers and novels were strewn around him. He was smoking a long-stemmed meerschaum pipe and on the bedside table, within arm's reach, was a litre of white wine and a glass.

'It's his legs,' explained Léontine. 'Since he got crushed between two buffers. He used to work for the railway. His bones are all shattered.'

Lace curtains subdued the light and two pots of geraniums brightened up the window-sill.

'I've read all the stories about you, Monsieur Maigret. I read all day long. I never used to read before. Bring a glass, Léontine.'

Maigret couldn't say no. He clinked glasses. Then, taking advantage of the fact that Léontine had stayed in the room, he pulled from his pocket the piece of lead piping he had asked permission to take away.

'Do you recognize this?'

Without becoming flustered, she said:

'Of course.'

'Where was it the last time you saw it?'

'On the big table in the lounge.'

'At Robert de Courçon's house?'

'At Monsieur's, yes. It comes from the outhouse, where some of the piping had to be replaced last winter when the water pipes froze and burst.'

'He kept that length of piping on the table?'

'There were all sorts of things. It was called a lounge, but it was the room where he lived all the time and where he worked.'

'You cleaned his house?'

'What he allowed me to do: I swept the floor and dusted
– as long as I didn't move any of his things! – and did the
washing-up.'

'Was he obsessive?'

'I didn't say that.'

'You can tell the inspector,' whispered her husband.

'I don't have any complaints about him.'

'Except that you hadn't been paid for months.'

'It's not his fault. If the others, over the road, had given
him the money they owed him . . .'

'Weren't you tempted to throw the piping away?'

'I tried. He ordered me to leave it there. He used it as a
paperweight. I recall him saying that it could come in useful
if burglars tried to break into the house. That was a strange
notion, because there were lots of guns on the walls. He
collected them.'

'Is it true, inspector, that his nephew killed himself?'

'It is true.'

'Do you think it was him? Another glass of wine? Me, you
see, as I was saying to my wife, the rich, I don't try to understand them. They don't think, they don't feel the way we do.'

'Do you know the Vernoux family?'

'Like everyone else, from passing them in the street. I've
heard people saying they had no money left, and they even
borrowed from their servants, and that must be true because
Léontine's boss wasn't getting his allowance any more and
couldn't pay her.'

His wife was signalling to him not to talk so much. He
didn't actually have a lot to say, but he was glad to have

company and to meet Detective Chief Inspector Maigret in the flesh.

Maigret left with the acrid taste of the white wine in his mouth. On the way back, he came across some life. Boys and girls on bicycles were returning to the villages, while families from the town were making their way slowly home.

At the law courts, they were probably still conferring in the magistrate's chambers. Maigret had declined to join them, because he didn't want to influence the decision they were going to make.

Would they resolve to close the investigation in the light of the doctor's suicide, taking it as an admission of guilt?

It was likely, and in that case, Chabot would feel remorse for the rest of his life.

When he reached Rue Clemenceau and gazed all the way down it to Rue de la République, the streets looked almost crowded: people were strolling along both pavements, others were coming out of the cinema, and every chair was taken on the terrace of the Café de la Poste. The sky already had the rosy glow of sunset.

He headed towards Place Viète, walking past his friend's house where he glimpsed Madame Chabot at an upstairs window. In Rue Rabelais, curious onlookers were still lingering around the Vernoux's home but, perhaps because death had visited the house, they kept a respectful distance, most of them on the opposite pavement.

Maigret told himself again that this case was none of his business, that he had a train to catch that evening, that he risked annoying everyone and falling out with his friend.

After which, unable to resist, he reached for the door knocker. He had to wait for a long time, watched by the onlookers, until at last he heard footsteps and the manservant opened the door a fraction.

'I should like to see Monsieur Hubert Vernoux.'

'Monsieur is not at home.'

Maigret entered uninvited. The hall was gloomy. There wasn't a sound to be heard.

'Is he in his apartment?'

'I think he is in bed.'

'One question: do your bedroom windows overlook the street?'

The manservant looked uncomfortable and spoke in an undertone.

'Yes. On the third floor. My wife and I sleep in the attic rooms.'

'And can you see the house opposite?'

Although they hadn't heard anything, the drawing-room door opened and Maigret recognized the silhouette of the sister-in-law standing in the doorway.

'What is it, Arsène?'

She had seen Maigret, but did not address him directly.

'I was telling Inspector Maigret that Monsieur is not at home.'

She eventually turned to him.

'Did you wish to speak to my brother-in-law?'

She resigned herself to opening the door a little wider.

'Come in.'

She was alone in the vast drawing room with closed curtains; a single lamp was lit on a pedestal table. No book was lying open, no newspaper, no needlework or tapestry. She must have been sitting there doing nothing when he had knocked.

'I can see you in his stead.'

'He's the person I wish to speak to.'

'Even if you go to his apartment, he probably won't be in a state to answer you.'

She walked towards the table on which stood a number of bottles and grabbed one which had contained Marc de Bourgogne and was now empty.

'This was half-full at lunchtime. He was in this room for only fifteen minutes while we were still at the table.'

'Does this happen often?'

'Nearly every day. Now he'll sleep until five or six o'clock and then his vision will be blurred. My sister and I have tried to lock up the bottles, but he always finds a way of getting at them. It's better that it should happen here than in some dreadful bar.'

'Does he sometimes frequent bars?'

'How should we know? He sneaks out through the back door, and later, when we see his bulging eyes and he starts stuttering, we know what it means. He'll end up like his father.'

'Has it been going on for long?'

'Years. Maybe he drank before too, but it had less effect on him. He doesn't look his age, but he is sixty-seven, after all.'

'I'm going to ask the servant to take me to him.'

'Wouldn't you rather come back later?'

'I'm leaving for Paris this evening.'

She realized there was no point arguing and pressed a bell. Arsène appeared:

'Show Inspector Maigret to Monsieur's rooms.'

Arsène looked at her in surprise, as if doubting her wisdom.

'Whatever will be will be!'

Without the manservant, Maigret would have got lost in the intersecting corridors, wide and echoing like those of a convent. He caught a glimpse of a kitchen full of gleaming copper pans. Like at Gros-Noyer, a bottle of white wine stood on the table, most likely Arsène's.

The manservant seemed utterly bemused by Maigret's attitude. After the question about his room, he had been expecting a real grilling. But Maigret asked him nothing.

In the right wing of the ground floor, he knocked on a carved oak door.

'It's me, Monsieur!' he said, raising his voice so as to be heard inside.

And, since they could hear a grunt:

'The inspector's with me and he insists on seeing you.'

They stood still while someone stomped up and down inside the room and finally opened the door a crack.

The sister-in-law hadn't been mistaken when she had talked about bulging eyes: they stared at Maigret in a sort of stupor.

'It's you!' stuttered Hubert Vernoux, slurring his words.

He must have gone to bed fully dressed. His clothes were crumpled, his white hair flopped over his forehead and he ran his hand through it mechanically.

'What do you want?'

'I wanted to have a conversation with you.'

It was hard to throw him out. Vernoux stepped aside, as if he hadn't yet fully come to his senses. The room was vast, and there was a very dark, ornate wooden four-poster bed with faded silk hangings.

All the furniture was antique, in more or less the same style, reminiscent of a chapel or a sacristy.

'Would you excuse me?'

Vernoux went into a bathroom, filled a glass of water and gargled. When he returned, he was already a little better.

'Have a seat. In this armchair if you like. Have you seen anyone?'

'Your sister-in-law.'

'Did she tell you I'd been drinking?'

'She showed me the bottle of Marc.'

He shrugged.

'It's always the same old thing. Women can't understand. A man who has suddenly been told that his son . . .'

His eyes misted over. His tone became quieter, whining.

'It's a hard blow, inspector. Especially when you only have the one son. What's his mother doing?'

'No idea.'

'She will declare that she's ill. That's her thing. She declares she's ill and no one dares say anything to her. Do you understand? Then her sister steps in: she calls it taking the house in hand . . .'

He reminded Maigret of an old actor who is determined at all costs to stir his audience's emotions. His slightly puffy face changed expression at a remarkable speed. Within a few minutes, his mobile features had successively displayed boredom, a degree of fear, then paternal sorrow and bitterness towards the two women. Now, fear resurfaced.

'Why were you so keen to see me?'

Maigret, who had not sat down in the armchair, pulled the length of piping out of his pocket and laid it on the table.

'Did you often go to your brother-in-law's house?'

'Around once a month to take him his money. I imagine people knew that I gave him money to get by?'

'So you noticed this piece of piping on his desk?'

He hesitated, grasping that the answer to this question was crucial, and he knew he had to make a quick decision.

'I think so.'

'It's the only physical clue that we have in this case. So far, no one seems to have grasped its full importance.'

He sat down, took his pipe out of his pocket and filled it. Vernoux remained on his feet, his features drawn as if he were suffering a violent headache.

'Have you got a few minutes?'

Without waiting for the reply, he went on:

'It was stated that the three murders were more or less identical, but in fact the first was very different from the other two. The widow Gibon and Gobillard were killed in cold blood, with premeditation. The man who rang the doorbell of the former midwife had gone there to kill her, and did so right away, in the hall. On the doorstep, he was already holding his weapon. When, two days later, he attacked Gobillard, he might not have been targeting him in particular, but he was out in the street with the intention of killing. Are you with me?'

Vernoux, in any case, was making an almost painful effort to fathom what Maigret was trying to get at.

'The Courçon case is different. On entering his house, the murderer did not have a weapon, so we can conclude that he did not go there with homicidal intentions. Something happened that drove him to act. Perhaps Courçon's attitude, which could often be provocative, perhaps even a threatening gesture on his part?'

Maigret broke off to strike a match and draw on his pipe.

'What do you think?'

'About what?'

'About my reasoning.'

'I thought this business was over.'

'Even if it is, I'm trying to understand.'

'A madman wouldn't bother himself with those considerations.'

'And supposing it weren't a madman, or at least, not a madman in the usual sense of the word? Bear with me for a little longer. Someone goes to Robert de Courçon's house, in the evening, quite openly, because he doesn't have any evil intentions, and, for reasons we don't know, is provoked into killing him. He leaves no trace and takes away the weapon, which indicates that he doesn't want to get caught.

'So it's a man who knows the victim, who's in the habit of going to see him at that time.

'It's inevitable that the police will follow that line of reasoning.

'And there's every chance that they'll find the culprit.'

Vernoux looked at him as if deep in thought, weighing up the pros and the cons.

'Let us now suppose that another murder is committed, at the other end of town, on someone who has nothing to do either with the murderer or with Courçon. What will happen?'

Vernoux did not completely suppress a smile. Maigret went on:

'The police would no longer *necessarily* look among the relatives of the first victim. They would all think that they must be dealing with a madman.'

He paused.

'That's what happened. And as an additional precaution, to reinforce this hypothesis of madness, the murderer killed a third time, in the street this time, picking on the first drunkard he came across. The magistrate, the prosecutor and the police were all hoodwinked.'

'Not you?'

'I wasn't alone in not believing it. Public opinion can sometimes be wrong. Often too, it has the same sort of intuition as women and children.'

'You mean it pointed the finger at my son?'

'It pointed the finger at this house.'

Saying no more, Maigret rose and went over to a Louis XIII table that served as a desk and on which some writing paper lay on a blotter. He took a sheet and pulled a piece of paper from his pocket.

'Arsène wrote,' he said casually.

'My manservant?'

Vernoux hurried over and Maigret noticed that despite his corpulence, he had the lightness that is common among some large men.

'He wanted to be questioned. But he didn't dare come to the police or the law courts of his own accord.'

'Arsène doesn't know anything.'

'That is possible, although his room overlooks the street.'

'Have you talked to him?'

'Not yet. I wonder whether he bears you a grudge for not paying his wages and borrowing money from him.'

'You know about that as well?'

'And you, Monsieur Vernoux, don't you have anything to say to me?'

'What would I say to you? My son—'

'Let's not talk about your son. I presume that you've never been happy?'

He did not answer, but stared at the carpet with its dark leaf pattern.

'As long as you had money, the satisfactions of vanity were enough. After all, you were the town's wealthy magnate.'

'These are personal matters which I have no wish to discuss.'

'Have you lost a lot of money these past few years?'

Maigret adopted a lighter tone, as if what he was saying were unimportant.

'Contrary to what you think, the investigation is not over and the case is still open. Until now, for reasons that do not concern me, the investigation has not been conducted by the book. We cannot put off questioning your servants any longer. We would also like to inquire into your affairs, examine your bank statements. We will find out what everyone has known for years, that you are battling in vain to salvage what remains of your fortune. Behind the façade there is nothing left, other than a man treated with contempt by his own family since he is no longer capable of making money.'

Hubert Vernoux opened his mouth. Maigret did not let him speak.

'They'll also call on psychiatrists.'

He saw Vernoux raise his head abruptly.

'I don't know what their opinion will be. I am not here officially. I'm going back to Paris this evening and my friend Chabot remains in charge of the investigation.

'I told you earlier that the first murder wasn't necessarily the work of a madman. I added that the other two had been committed with a specific aim, following a fairly perverse logic.

'But I shouldn't be surprised if the psychiatrists consider that logic as a sign of madness, of a particular sort of madness, one more common than people think, which they call paranoia.

'You must have read the books that your son was bound to have in his study?'

'I have glanced at some of them.'

'You ought to re-read them.'

'You're not claiming that I—'

'I'm not claiming anything. I watched you playing cards yesterday and I saw you win. You must be convinced that you will win this game in the same way.'

'I'm not playing any game.'

He protested feebly, inwardly flattered that Maigret should pay him so much attention and indirectly acknowledge his ingenuity.

'I must warn you against one mistake you should avoid making: it won't help matters at all – quite the contrary – if there is any further carnage, or even a single murder. Do you understand me? As your son kept saying, madness has its rules, its own logic.'

Once again, Vernoux opened his mouth, but Maigret still wouldn't allow him to speak.

'I've finished. I'm taking the nine-thirty train and I have to go and pack before dinner.'

Nonplussed and disappointed, Vernoux stared at him uncomprehendingly and made a move to stop him, but Maigret was already striding towards the door.

'I'll find my own way out.'

It took him a while, but eventually he came to the kitchen. Arsène burst out of the room, a quizzical look in his eye.

Maigret said nothing, followed the main corridor, opened the front door himself and the manservant closed it after him.

Only three or four stalwarts were left on the pavement opposite. Would the vigilantes be out on patrol again tonight?

He nearly headed in the direction of the law courts, where the meeting was probably still going on, but decided to do as he had said and go and pack his suitcase. Once in the street, he fancied a glass of beer and he sat down at a terrace table at the Café de la Poste.

Everyone stared at him. People spoke in hushed voices. Some began to whisper.

He drank two large beers, slowly, savouring them, as if he was in a Parisian café on the boulevards, and parents stopped to point him out to their children.

He saw Chalus, the school teacher, walk past in the company of a paunchy character to whom he was telling a story involving a great deal of gesticulation. Chalus didn't see Maigret and the two men disappeared around the corner.

It was almost dark and the terrace had emptied when he rose laboriously to make his way to Chabot's house. His friend opened the door, shooting him an anxious look.

'I was wondering where you were.'

'Sitting at the terrace of a café.'

He hung his hat on the coat stand and caught sight of the table laid for dinner in the dining room, but dinner wasn't ready and Chabot showed him into his study.

After a fairly lengthy silence, Chabot muttered, without looking at Maigret:

'The investigation is continuing.'

He seemed to be saying: 'You've won. You see! We're not as spineless as you thought.'

Maigret didn't smile, but gave a little nod of approval.

'As of now, the house in Rue Rabelais is under police guard. Tomorrow I shall question the servants.'

'By the way, I forgot to return this to you.'

'Are you really leaving tonight?'

'I have to.'

'I wonder whether we'll reach a successful conclusion.'

Maigret had placed the lead piping on the table and was rummaging in his pockets for Arsène's letter.

'Louise Sabati?' he asked.

'Apparently she's out of danger. The vomiting saved her. She had just eaten and hadn't begun digesting.'

'What did she say?'

'She answers in monosyllables.'

'Did she know they were both going to die?'

'Yes.'

'Did she accept it?'

'He told her that they would never be allowed to be happy.'

'He didn't talk to her about the three murders?'

'No.'

'Or about his father?'

Chabot looked him in the eyes.

'Do you think it's him?'

Maigret merely blinked.

'Is he mad?'

'The psychiatrists will decide.'

'In your view?'

'I will gladly say that sane people do not kill. But that is simply an opinion.'

'Not very orthodox, maybe?'

'No.'

'You seem preoccupied.'

'I'm waiting.'

'What?'

'For something to happen.'

'Do you think something's going to happen today?'

'I hope so.'

'Why?'

'Because I paid a visit to Hubert Vernoux.'

'Did you tell him—'

'I told him how and why the three murders were committed. I told him how the murderer would be expected to react.'

Chabot, so proud earlier of the decision he had taken, once again looked stricken.

'But . . . in that case . . . aren't you afraid that—'

'Dinner is served,' announced Rose, while Madame Chabot, who was making her way to the dining room, smiled at them.

9. *Vintage Napoleon Brandy*

Once again, because of the old lady, they had to keep quiet, or rather only talk of casual matters unrelated to their concerns, and, that evening, the talk was of food, in particular the best way to cook hare *à la royale*.

Madame Chabot had made profiteroles again and Maigret ate five, nauseated, his gaze fixed on the hands of the ancient clock.

By 8.30 still nothing had happened.

'There's no hurry. I've ordered a taxi to go and pick up your luggage from the hotel first.'

'I have to go there anyway to pay my bill.'

'I telephoned and told them to put it on my account. That will teach you not to stay with us when, once every twenty years, you deign to come to Fontenay.'

Coffee and brandy were served. Maigret accepted a cigar, because it was the tradition and his friend's mother would have been offended if he had refused.

It was 8.55 and the taxi was outside the door, its engine running and the driver waiting, when the telephone finally rang.

Chabot dashed over and picked up the receiver.

'Speaking, yes . . . What? . . . He's dead? . . . I can't hear you, Féron . . . Stop shouting . . . Yes . . . I'm on my way . . . Have him taken to the hospital, it goes without saying . . .'

He turned to Maigret.

'I have to go up there right away. Do you absolutely have to return to Paris tonight?'

'Without fail.'

'I won't be able to come to the station with you.'

Because of his mother, he said no more, grabbed his hat and his lightweight coat.

Only when they were outside did he mutter:

'There's been another terrible scene at the Vernoux's. Hubert Vernoux, blind drunk, started vandalizing his room, and in the end went completely berserk and slashed his wrist with his razor.'

Maigret's calm surprised him.

'He's not dead,' added Chabot.

'I know.'

'How do you know?'

'Because people like that don't commit suicide.'

'But his son—'

'Go on. They're waiting for you.'

The station was only five minutes away. Maigret walked up to the taxi.

'We should just make it,' said the driver.

Maigret turned one last time towards his friend, who looked bewildered standing there on the pavement.

'Write to me.'

It was a tedious journey. At two or three stations, Maigret alighted to have a drink, and he eventually dozed off, vaguely aware, at each stop, of the stationmaster's announcements and the creaking of the carriages.

He reached Paris in the small hours and a taxi drove him home where, from below, he smiled at the open window. His wife was waiting for him on the landing.

'Not too tired? Did you get some sleep?'

He drank three large cups of coffee before relaxing.

'Do you want a bath?'

Of course he was going to have one! It was good to hear Madame Maigret's voice and rediscover the smell of the apartment, with the furniture and objects in their place.

'I didn't understand what you said to me on the telephone. Were you on a case?'

'It's finished.'

'What was it?'

'A man who couldn't bear to lose.'

'I don't understand.'

'It doesn't matter. There are people who are capable of absolutely anything rather than taking a tumble.'

'Only you know what you mean,' she murmured philosophically, without worrying about it any further.

At 9.30, in the chief's office, he was briefed about the disappearance of the politician's daughter. It was an ugly business, with orgies in a basement and drugs to boot.

'It's almost sure that she didn't leave of her own free will, and there's little chance that she was kidnapped. The most likely scenario is that she took a drug overdose and her friends panicked and got rid of the body.'

Maigret copied out a list of names and addresses.

'Lucas has already questioned some of them. So far, no one has been willing to talk.'

Wasn't it his job to get people to talk?

'Had fun?'

'Where?'

'In Bordeaux.'

'It rained every day.'

He didn't mention Fontenay. He barely had the time to think about it over the next three days, which he spent extracting confessions from young idiots who thought they were smart.

Then, among his mail, he found a letter postmarked Fontenay-le-Comte. He already more or less knew how the case had ended from the newspapers.

Chabot, in his neat, compact, slightly pointed handwriting, which could have been mistaken for a woman's, filled in the details.

At some point, shortly after you had left Rue Rabelais, he sneaked into the cellar and Arsène saw him come up with a bottle of vintage Napoleon brandy that the Courçon family had kept for two generations.

Maigret couldn't help smiling. For his last binge, Hubert Vernoux hadn't been content with any old drink! He had chosen the rarest bottle in the house, a venerable bottle that they kept rather like a testimony of their nobility.

When Arsène went in to inform him that dinner was served, his eyes were already wild and red-rimmed. He commanded him theatrically to leave him alone, shouting: 'Let the bitches eat without me!'

They sat down at the table. Around ten minutes later, thuds were heard coming from his apartment. They sent Arsène up to see what was going on, but the door was locked, and Vernoux was smashing everything he could lay his hands on, yelling obscenities.

Once they realized what was happening, his sister-in-law suggested:

'The window . . .'

They didn't trouble themselves, but remained at the table while Arsène went out into the courtyard. A window was half-open. He drew back the curtains. Vernoux saw him. He was already holding a razor.

He shouted again that he wanted to be left alone, that he'd had enough and, according to Arsène, continued to use vile language of a kind that no one had ever heard him utter before.

Not daring to enter the room, Arsène called for help, but meanwhile Vernoux began to slash his wrist. Blood spurted out. Vernoux looked at it in horror, and after that, allowed himself to be taken care of. A few moments later, he crumpled on to the rug in a faint.

Since then, he has refused to answer any questions. At the hospital the next day, they found him busy ripping open his mattress and they had to lock him in a padded cell.

Desprez, the psychiatrist, came from Niort to assess him, and tomorrow he'll be seeing a specialist from Poitiers.

In Desprez's opinion, there is hardly any doubt about Vernoux's madness, but he would rather take every precaution, given that the case has caused a huge stir locally.

I issued the burial permit for Alain. The funeral is tomorrow. The Sabati girl is still in hospital and is absolutely fine. I don't know what to do with her. Her father must be working somewhere or other, but no one is able to get hold of him. I can't send her back to her rooms, because she still has suicidal thoughts.

My mother is talking about taking her on as a maid to help Rose, who is getting older. I fear that people . . .

Maigret didn't have time to read to the end of the letter that morning because a key witness was brought in. He stuffed it in his pocket. What became of it he never knew.

'By the way,' he said to his wife the same evening, 'I had some news from Julien Chabot.'

'What does he say?'

He looked for the letter, but couldn't find it. It must have fallen out of his pocket when he had taken out his handkerchief or his tobacco pouch.

'They're going to hire a new maid.'

'Is that all?'

'More or less.'

A long time afterwards, gazing worriedly at his reflection in the mirror, he muttered:

'I found him aged.'

'Who are you talking about?'

'Chabot.'

'How old is he?'

'The same age as me, give or take a couple of months.'

Madame Maigret tidied the room, as she always did before going to bed.

'He should have married,' she declared.

OTHER TITLES IN THE SERIES

Pietr the Latvian

The Late Monsieur Gallet

The Hanged Man of Saint-Pholien

The Carter of *La Providence*

The Yellow Dog

Night at the Crossroads

A Crime in Holland

The Grand Banks Café

A Man's Head

The Dancer at the Gai-Moulin

The Two-Penny Bar

The Shadow Puppet

The Saint-Fiacre Affair

Mr Hire's Engagement

The Flemish House

The Madman of Bergerac

The Misty Harbour

Liberty Bar

Lock No. 1

Maigret

Cécile is Dead

The Cellars of the Majestic

The Judge's House

Signed, Picpus

Inspector Cadaver

Félicie

Maigret Gets Angry

Maigret in New York

Maigret's Holiday

Maigret's Dead Man

Maigret's First Case

My Friend Maigret

Maigret at the Coroner's

Maigret and the Old Lady

Madame Maigret's Friend

Maigret's Memoirs

Maigret at Picratt's

Maigret Takes a Room

Maigret and the Tall Woman

Maigret, Lognon and the Gangsters

Maigret's Revolver

Maigret and the Man on the Bench

Maigret is Afraid

Maigret's Mistake

Maigret Goes to School

And more to follow